A PUFFIN BOOK

PROPERTY OF

_____

_____

WENDY COOLING taught English in London secondary schools for many years before moving to BookTrust, a charity that supports reading to children and adults. There she created the Bookstart project giving books to babies to encourage parents and carers to share books from the very beginning. Wendy has edited many short story and poetry anthologies for children, and continues to travel the world talking about children's books and reading. She was honoured to receive an MBE from the Queen and an Eleanor Farjeon Award for services to children's literature. Wendy lives in London – and she still loves reading!

Stories chosen by
WENDY COOLING

The PUFFIN BOOK of Christmas Stories

A PUFFIN BOOK

PUFFIN BOOKS

UK | USA | Canada | Ireland | Australia
India | New Zealand | South Africa

Puffin Books is part of the Penguin Random House group of companies
whose addresses can be found at global.penguinrandomhouse.com.

www.penguin.co.uk
www.puffin.co.uk
www.ladybird.co.uk

First published 2001
This edition published 2019
001

The acknowledgements on pages 161–163 constitute an extension of this copyright page

Set in 12.5/16.5 pt Sabon LT Std
Typeset by Jouve (UK), Milton Keynes
Printed and bound in Great Britain by Clays Ltd, Elcograf S.p.A.

A CIP catalogue record for this book is available from the British Library

ISBN: 978–0–241–37717–8

All correspondence to:
Puffin Books
Penguin Random House Children's
80 Strand, London WC2R ORL

MIX
Paper from
responsible sources
FSC® C018179
www.fsc.org

Penguin Random House is committed to a
sustainable future for our business, our readers
and our planet. This book is made from Forest
Stewardship Council® certified paper.

Contents

Contents

The Christmas Party

from *A Northern Childhood*, set in 1976

GEORGE LAYTON

OUR CLASSROOM looked smashing. Lots of silver tinsel and crepe paper and lanterns. *We'd* made the lanterns, but Miss Taylor had bought the rest herself, out of her own money. Oh, only today and tomorrow and then we break up. Mind you, if school was like this all the time, I wouldn't be bothered about breaking up. Putting up Christmas decorations and playing games – much better than doing writing and spelling any day. I watched the snow coming down outside. Smashing! More sliding tomorrow. I love

Christmas. I wish it was more than once a year. Miss Taylor started tapping on the blackboard with a piece of chalk. Everybody was talking and she kept on tapping until the only person you could hear was Norbert Lightowler.

'Look if I get a six and land on you, you get knocked off and I still get another go!'

The whole class was looking at him.

'Look, when Colin got a six, he landed on *me* and *he* got another . . .!'

Suddenly he realized that he was the only one talking and he started going red.

'Thank you, Norbert, I think we all know the rules of Ludo.'

Miss Taylor can be right sarcastic sometimes. Everybody laughed. Even Miss Taylor smiled.

'Now, since it is getting so noisy, we're going to stop these games and do some work.'

Everybody groaned and Tony and me booed – quietly so Miss Taylor couldn't hear. She hates people that boo. She says people who boo are cowards.

'Who is that booing?'

We must have been booing louder than we thought.

'Who is that booing?'

Miss Taylor looked at Tony. I looked at Tony. They both looked at me. I put my hand up.

'It was me, Miss.'

Tony put his hand up.

'It was me an' all, Miss.'

She looked at us.

'You both know what I think of booing, don't you?'

We nodded.

'Yes, Miss.'

'Yes, Miss.'

'Don't ever let me hear it again.'

We shook our heads.

'No, Miss.'

'No, Miss.'

She turned to the class.

'Now, the work I have in mind is discussion work.'

Everybody groaned again, except me and Tony.

'I thought we'd discuss tomorrow's Christmas party!'

We all cheered and Miss Taylor smiled. We have a Christmas party every year, the whole school together in the main hall. Each class has its own table and we all bring the food from home.

'Now, does everybody know what they're bringing from home for the party tomorrow?'

I knew. I was bringing a jelly. I put my hand up.

'I'm bringing a jelly, Miss!'

Everybody started shouting at once and Miss Taylor moved her hands about to calm us down.

'All right, all right, one at a time. Don't get excited. Jennifer Greenwood, what are you bringing?'

Jennifer Greenwood was sitting in the back row next to Valerie Burns.

'C'mon, Jennifer, what are you bringing for tomorrow?'

She put her hand up.

'Please, Miss, I'm bringing a custard trifle, Miss.'

Norbert Lightowler pulled his mouth into a funny shape and pretended to be sick.

'Ugh, I hate custard. I'm not gonna have any of that!'

Everybody laughed, except Miss Taylor.

'Well, Norbert, if I was Jennifer I wouldn't dream of giving you any. Right, Jennifer?'

Jennifer just giggled with Valerie Burns. Norbert was looking down at his desk.

'And, Norbert, what are you bringing tomorrow?'

'Polony sandwiches, Miss, my mum's making 'em, and a bottle of mixed pickles, Miss, homemade!'

Miss Taylor said that would be lovely, and carried on asking right round the class. Tony said that he was bringing a Christmas cake. I was bringing the jelly that my mum was going to make, and Colin Wilkinson was bringing some currant buns. Valerie Burns said that she was bringing some lemon curd tarts, and Freda Holdsworth called her a spiteful cat because *she* was bringing the lemon curd tarts, and Valerie Burns *knew* she was bringing lemon curd tarts because she'd told her and she was a blooming copycat. Anyway Miss Taylor calmed her down by saying that it was a good job they were both bringing lemon curd tarts, because then there would be enough for everybody, and everybody would want one, wouldn't they? And she asked everybody who would want a lemon curd tart to put their hands up, and everybody put their hands up. Even I put my hand up and I hate lemon curd. Well, it *was* Christmas.

After everybody had told Miss Taylor what they were bringing, she said that there'd be enough for the whole school, never mind just our class, but we should remember that Christmas isn't just for eating and parties, and she asked Tony what the most important thing about Christmas is.

'Presents, Miss!'

'No, Tony, not presents. Christmas is when the baby Jesus was born, and that is the most important thing, and when you're all enjoying your presents and parties this year, you must all remember that. Will you all promise me?'

Everybody promised that they'd remember Jesus and then Miss Taylor started asking us all how we were going to spend Christmas. Freda Holdsworth said she was going to Bridlington on Christmas Eve to stay with her cousin, and on Christmas Eve they'd both put their stockings up for Father Christmas, but before they'd go to bed, they'd leave a glass of milk and some biscuits for him in case he was hungry. Norbert Lightowler said that that's daft because there's no such thing as Father Christmas. Some of the others agreed, but most of them said course there is. I just wasn't sure. What I can't understand is, that if there *is* a Father Christmas, how does he get round everybody in one night? I mean the presents must come from somewhere, but how can he do it all by himself? And Norbert said how can there be only *one* Father Christmas, when he'd seen *two* down in town in Baldwin Street and another outside the fish market, and Neville Bastowe said he'd seen one in Dickenson's. Well, what about the one my mum had taken me to see at the Co-op? He'd promised to bring me a racer.

'Please, Miss, there's one at the Co-op an' all. He's promised to bring me a racer.'

And then Miss Taylor explained that all these others are Father Christmas's brothers and relations who help out because he's so busy and Freda Holdsworth said Miss Taylor was right, and Norbert said he'd never thought of that, but that Paul Hopwood, he's in 2B, had told him that Father Christmas is just his dad dressed up, and I said that that's daft and it couldn't be because Father Christmas comes to our house every year and I haven't got a dad, and Miss Taylor said that if those who didn't believe in Father Christmas didn't get any presents, they'd only have themselves to blame, and I agreed! Then she asked me what I'd be doing on Christmas Day.

'Well, Miss, when I wake up in the morning, I'll look round and see what presents I've got, and I'll play with them and I'll empty my stocking, and usually there are some sweets so I'll eat them, and when I've played a bit more I'll go and wake my mum up and show her what I've got, and then I'll wake my Auntie Doreen – she always stays with us every Christmas; and then after breakfast I'll play a bit more, and then we'll have Christmas dinner, and then we'll go to my grandad's and I'll play a bit more there, and then I'll go home to bed, and that'll be the end!'

Miss Taylor said that all sounded very nice and she hoped everybody would have such a nice Christmas, but she was surprised I wasn't going to church. Well, I told her that there wouldn't really be time because my grandad likes us to be there early to hear Wilfred Pickles on the wireless visiting a hospital, and to listen to the Queen talking, and then the bell went for home-time and Miss Taylor said we could all go quietly and told us not to forget our stuff for the party.

I went with Tony to get our coats from the cloakroom. Everybody was talking about the party and Barry was there shouting out that their class was going to have the best table because their teacher had made them a Christmas pudding with money in it! I told him that was nothing because Miss Taylor had given everybody in our class sixpence, but he didn't believe me.

'Gerraway, you bloomin' fibber.'

'She did, didn't she, Tony?'

Tony shook his head.

'Did she heckers like – she wouldn't give 'owt away.'

Huh! You'd think Tony'd've helped me kid Barry along.

'Well, she bought all our Christmas decorations for the classroom . . .' and I went to get my coat. I took my gloves out of my pocket and they were still soaking wet from snowballing at playtime, so I thought I'd put them on the pipes to dry.

'Hey, Tony, my gloves are still sodden.'

'Well, put 'em on the pipes.'

'Yeh, that's a good idea.'

While they dried I sat on the pipes. Ooh, it was lovely and warm. There's a window above the basins and I could see the snow was still coming down, really thickly now.

'Hey, it isn't half going to be deep tomorrow.'

Everybody had gone now except for Barry, Tony and me. Tony was standing on the basins looking out of the window and Barry was doing up his coat. It has a hood on it. I wish I had one like it. I could see through the door into the main hall where the Christmas tree was. It looked lovely. Ever so big. It was nearly up to the ceiling.

'Hey, isn't it a big Christmas tree?' Tony jumped down from the basin and came over to where I was sitting.

'Yeh. It's smashing. All them coloured balls. Isn't it lovely, eh, Barry?'

Barry came over.

'Not bad. C'mon you two, let's get going, eh?'

'Just a sec, let's see if my gloves are dry.'

They weren't really but I put them on. As I was fastening my coat, Barry said how about going carol singing to get a bit of money.

Tony was quite keen, but I didn't know. I mean, my mum'd be expecting me home round about now.

'I suppose *you* can't come because your mum'll be cross with you, as usual!'

Huh. It's all right for Barry. His mum and dad aren't bothered where he goes.

'Course I'll come. Where do you want to go?'

Barry said down near the woods where the posh live, but Tony said it was useless there because they never gave you nowt. So we decided to go round Belgrave Road way, where it's only *quite* posh. It takes about ten minutes to get to Belgrave Road from our school and on the way we argued about which carols to sing. I wanted

'Away in a Manger' but Barry wanted 'O Come all Ye Faithful'.

' "Away in a Manger" isn't half as good as "O Come all Ye Faithful", is it, Tony?'

Tony shrugged his shoulders.

'I quite like "Once in Royal David's City".'

In the end we decided to take it in turns to choose. Belgrade Road's ever so long and we started at number three with 'O Come all Ye Faithful'.

'O Come all ye faithful, joyful and trium . . .'

That was as far as we got. A bloke opened the door, gave us three halfpence and told us to push off.

Tony was disgusted.

'That's a good start, halfpenny each.'

Barry told him to stop grumbling.

'It's better than nothing. C'mon.'

We went on to number five and Tony and Barry started quarrelling again because Tony said it was his turn to choose, but Barry wanted his go again because we'd only sung one line. So we did 'O Come all Ye Faithful' again.

'O come all ye faithful, joyful and triumphant, O . . .'

We didn't get any further this time either. An old lady opened the door and said her mother was poorly so could we sing a bit quieter. We started once more but she stopped us again and said it was still just a little bit too loud and could we sing it quieter.

'O come all ye faithful, joyful and triumphant, O come ye, O come ye to Be–eth–lehem . . .'

And we sang the whole thing like that, in whispers. We could hardly hear each other. I felt daft and started giggling and that set Tony and Barry off, but the old lady didn't seem to notice. She just stood there while we sang and when we finished she said thank you and gave us twopence each.

At the next house we sang 'Once in Royal David's City' right through and then rang the doorbell, but nobody came. We missed number nine out because it was empty and up for sale, and at number eleven we sang 'Away in a Manger'.

We went to the end of the road singing every carol we knew. We must've made about a pound between us by the time we got to the other end, and Barry said how about going back and doing the other side of the road. I was all for it, but I just happened to see St Chad's clock. Bloomin' heck! Twenty to nine! I couldn't believe it. I thought it'd be about half-past six, if that. Twenty to nine!

'Hey, I'd better get going. It's twenty to nine. My mum'll kill me!'

The other two said they were going to do a bit more carol singing, so they gave me my share of the money and I ran home as fast as I could. I took a short cut through the snicket behind the fish and chip shop and I got home in about five minutes. I could see my mum standing outside the front door talking to Mrs Theabould, our next-door neighbour. She saw me and walked towards me. I tried to act all calm as if it was only about half-past five or six o'clock.

'Hello, Mum, I've been carol singing.'

She gave me a clout. She nearly knocked me over. Right on my freezing cold ear an' all.

'Get inside, you! I've been going mad with worry. Do you know what time it is? Nine o'clock. Get inside!'

She pushed me inside and I heard her thank Mrs Theabould and come in after me. I thought she was going to give me another clout, but she just shouted at me, saying that I was lucky she didn't get the police out, and why didn't I tell her where I was? By this time I was crying my head off.

'But I was only bloomin' carol singing.'

'I'll give you carol singing. Get off to bed,' and she pushed me upstairs into my bedroom.

'But what about my jelly for tomorrow? Have you made it?'

I thought she was going to go mad.

'Jelly! I'll give you jelly. If you think I've nothing better to do than make jellies while you're out roaming the streets! Get to bed!'

'But I've told Miss Taylor I'm bringing a jelly. I've got to have one. Please, Mum.'

She just told me to wash my hands and face and get to bed.

'And if I hear another word out of you, you'll get such a good hiding, you'll wish you hadn't come home,' and she went downstairs.

I didn't dare say another word. What was I going to do about my jelly? I had to bring one. I'd promised. There was only one thing for it. I'd have to make one myself. So I decided to wait until my mum went to bed, and then I'd go downstairs and make one. I don't know how I kept awake. I'm sure I nodded off once or twice, but after a while I heard my mum switch her light out, and when I'd given her enough time to get to sleep, I crept downstairs.

I've seen my mum make jellies tons of times and I knew you had to have boiling water, so I put the kettle on. I looked in the cupboard for a jelly and at first I thought I'd had it, but I found one and emptied it into a glass bowl. It was a funny jelly. Not like the ones my mum usually has. It was sort of like a powder. Still, it said jelly on the packet, so it was all right. A new flavour most likely. I poured the hot water into a bowl, closed the cupboard door, switched off the light, and took the jelly upstairs and I put it under my bed. I could hear my mum snoring so I knew I was all right, and I went to sleep.

Next thing I heard was my mum shouting from downstairs.

'C'mon, get up or you'll be late for school.'

I got up and pulled the jelly from under the bed. It had set lovely. All wobbly. But it was a bit of a funny colour, sort of yellowy-white. Still I'd got my jelly and that's what mattered. My mum didn't say much when I got downstairs. She just told me to eat my breakfast and get to school, so I did. When I'd finished I put my coat on and said tarah to my mum in the kitchen and went off. But first I sneaked upstairs and got my jelly and wrapped it in a piece of newspaper.

The first thing we had to do at school was to take what we'd brought for the party into the main hall and stick on a label with our name on it and leave it on our table. Norbert Lightowler was there with his polony sandwiches and mixed pickles. So was Neville Bastowe. Neville Bastowe said that my jelly was a bit funny-looking, but Norbert said he loved jelly more than anything else and he could eat all the jellies in the world. Miss Taylor came along then and told us to take our coats off and go to our classroom. The party wasn't starting till twelve o'clock, so in the morning we played games and sang carols and Miss Taylor read us a story.

Then we had a long playtime and we had a snowball fight with 2B, and I went on the slides until old Wilkie, that's the caretaker, came and put ashes on the ice. Then the bell went and we all had to go to our tables in the main hall. At every place was a Christmas cracker, and everybody had a streamer, but Mr Dyson, the Headmaster, said that we couldn't throw any streamers until we'd finished eating. I pulled my cracker with Tony and got a red paper hat and a pencil sharpener. Tony got a blue hat and a small magnifying glass. When everybody had pulled their crackers we said grace and started eating. I started with a sausage roll that Neville Bastowe had brought, and a polony sandwich.

Miss Taylor had shared my jelly out in bowls and Jennifer Greenwood said it looked horrible and she wasn't going to have any. So did Freda Holdsworth. But Norbert was already on his jelly and said it was lovely and he'd eat anybody else's. Tony started his jelly and spat it out.

'Ugh, it's horrible.'

I tasted mine, and it *was* horrible, but I forced it down.

'It's not that bad.'

Just then Tony said he could see my mum.

'Isn't that your mum over there?'

He pointed to the door. She was talking to Miss Taylor and they both came over.

'Your mother says you forgot your jelly this morning, here it is.'

Miss Taylor put a lovely red jelly on the table. It had bananas and cream on it, and bits of orange. My mum asked me where I'd got my jelly from. I told her I'd made it. I thought she'd be cross, but she and Miss Taylor just laughed and told us to enjoy ourselves, and then my mum went off. Everybody put their hands up for a portion of my mum's jelly – except Norbert.

'I don't want any of that. This is lovely. What flavour is it?'

I told him it was a new flavour and I'd never heard of it before.

'Well, what's it called?'

'Aspic.'

'Y'what?'

'Aspic jelly – it's a new flavour!'[1]

Norbert ate the whole thing and was sick afterwards, and everybody else had some of my mum's. It was a right good party.

[1] Aspic is meaty savoury jelly which is definitely not suitable for children's parties!

The Silver Horse

Ursula Moray Williams

CHRISTMAS EVE and stars in the sky! Snow, snow everywhere, and the wide white world so quiet!

Inside the carpenter's shop six wooden hobby-horses stood beside the work bench, waiting for Santa Claus. One red, one blue, one green, one yellow, one purple and one white with spots, they all had round black eyes and scarlet wheels, of which they were very proud. Old Mr Tandy the carpenter had just finished making them.

Now he was tidying up his shop before going down the village street to eat a mince pie and drink a cup of tea with old Mrs Higgins. The Christmas bells were ringing. In two hours it would be midnight and he wanted company.

Far away across the fields came the galloping hooves of a silver horse. It was the Christmas horse with a bag on its back, gathering up the naughtiness the children had thrown away before Santa Claus came.

All the children had said their prayers and begged pardon for their badness during the year. Now they were fast asleep in bed with their stockings hung up, smiling in their sleep.

The Christmas horse came galloping down the street to stick his head over the half-door of the carpenter's shop.

'Oh, you beautiful thing!' cried the hobby-horses, clattering to welcome him.

'I can't stay to play with you!' said the silver horse. 'I have hundreds of miles to go! Happy Christmas to you all! Goodbye!'

Away he went down the village street.

'What a pity!' said the hobby-horses, listening to the flying feet.

The smallest of the hobby-horses had nibbled a hole in the bag on the back of the silver horse. He wanted to find out what was inside it. And something had got out!

There in the snow where the silver horse had stood was a small round creature with bright eyes and turned-out toes. It was a bundle of badness belonging to Little Mikey.

Little Mikey was a boy who always ran away. He ran away from home, he ran away from school. When Christmas time came he made up his mind never to run away again. He had said he was sorry and thrown his naughtiness out of the window. Now it had escaped out of the bag on the back of the silver horse.

'Come out and play!' said Little Mikey, dancing in the snow.

'No! No! No!' said the hobby-horses.

'Just a little frisk in the fields! Just a little gallop in the snow!' said Little Mikey. 'Hark at the Christmas bells! There's lots of time before Santa comes! Come out with me!'

'No! No!' said all the hobby-horses. 'Old Mr Tandy would be very angry!'

'He wouldn't know!' said Little Mikey. 'Come out and try your scarlet wheels! Come out and stretch your wooden legs! Come out and jump in the snow and slide on the ice!'

'No!' said the hobby-horses.

'Then I shall go after the silver horse,' said Little Mikey, 'but now I shall never catch him up! I have wasted my time talking to you and I shall be left behind and never see him again, unless one of you lets me ride on your back, but of course not one of you is as fast as he!' and the little creature began to sniff.

The hobby-horses came trotting out of the workshop. They were sorry to see Little Mikey sad, and every one of them wished to prove that he could catch up with the silver horse. The leader took Little Mikey on his back and they galloped like the wind up the quiet village street.

Old Mr Tandy the carpenter was just finishing his cup of tea.

'What was that?' he said to Mrs Higgins. 'The Christmas horse has already gone by and it is still too early for Santa Claus. I had better be getting back to my workshop!'

But when Mr Tandy got back to his workshop the door was wide open and the hobby-horses were gone! The poor old carpenter sat down with his head in his hands and cried.

Presently he wiped his eyes and blew his nose. 'Crying won't bring back my horses!' he said. 'I had better go and find them!'

He took a stick to walk with and a lantern off the peg to light his way. Then he tramped off up the village street to follow the hobby-horses and the silver horse.

Presently he had left the village behind, with all the lighted windows lit up by spangled Christmas trees. Frosty fields and woods stretched out before him, with snow-filled ditches and frozen streams.

The hobby-horses had left the road, and now their tracks led over hill and dale. They had jumped over hedges and leaped over ditches, and among the trails left by their scarlet wheels were the sharp clear hoof-prints of the silver horse.

Now and again Mr Tandy stooped down to pick up a fragment of broken braid, a wisp of mane torn by the branches, or even a battered wheel. Once he found a whole bridle hanging on a hedgerow, and the snow was stained with splinters of painted wood.

Old Mr Tandy tramped for miles, but he knew he would never catch up with the silver horse. Presently he turned round, and began slowly and painfully to make his way home again. His lantern went out, and his stick was broken, so he had to throw it away.

Half an hour before midnight he stumbled through the door and sat down to dry himself before a fire of wood-shavings. In a few minutes he was fast asleep.

Outside, the white world was quiet again under the snow, until far away across the fields came the galloping hooves of a silver horse. And with the galloping a tappeting and clattering as if wooden sticks were tapping and wooden wheels going round.

Nearer and nearer they came till they clattered down the village street. The workshop door was pushed open and the hobby-horses trotted in. Outside in the snow stood the silver horse whinnying a piercing whinny.

Old Mr Tandy woke with a start, and the first thing he saw was his six hobby-horses. But oh! what a state they were in! Their wheels were broken, their paint was scratched, their manes were torn and their legs were battered. And every one of them hung his head in shame and penitence. The silver horse had a hole in his bag and out of the bag were sticking the runaway legs of Little Mikey.

Old Mr Tandy did not stop to scold them. With his needle and thread he quickly stitched up the hole in case anything else should escape and cause mischief. Then he gave the silver horse a kindly clap on the back and away it galloped till the sound of its hooves could no longer be heard, while Mr Tandy set to work mending the reins and painting the legs and hammering new wheels on his hobby-horses, faster than he had worked in all his life before.

Two minutes before midnight the job was done, and only one thing was missing. The pretty red wheels they had all been so proud of had been replaced by plain white wooden ones. That was their punishment, and it would remind the hobby-horses never to run away again.

As the last wheel was fixed, the Christmas bells began to peal with a new and joyful sound, mingling with the tinkle of sleighbells and the patter of reindeer's feet.

Mr Tandy took his hobby-horses to the door. Then he kissed each one on the nose and stood waiting for Santa Claus and listening to the Christmas chimes across the sparkling snow, while the reindeer sleigh came nearer and nearer, and far, far away across the wide white world beyond the village galloped the silver horse.

Just Like an Angel

GILLIAN CROSS

GABRIEL WAS the youngest in the family, and he wasn't like his brothers. Michael, Richard and Edward were long-legged and cheerful, with blond hair and blue eyes, but Gabriel was small and shy. The others teased him about everything.

Especially angels.

It started when he was four. They were on their way to stay with Grandmother, for the Christmas carol service. As they drove into her village, Gabriel looked out of the car window and saw big, white shapes circling in the sky. They were moving slowly, with the winter sunlight glancing off their wings.

They weren't aeroplanes. Gabriel knew that aeroplanes moved faster, and made a noise. He lifted his hand and pointed.

'Look! Angels!'

Michael and Richard and Edward fell about laughing.

'Hey, Mum! Gabe thinks those are *angels*!'

'Leave him alone,' Mrs Jennings said. 'They're gliders, Gabriel. Like aeroplanes without engines. They ride on the air currents.'

Her voice was kind, but she was laughing too. She couldn't help it. As they drove up the main street of the village, she stopped at the petrol pumps, and told Mr King the garage man, speaking slowly and clearly, so that he could see what she was saying.

'Gabriel thought the gliders were angels.'

Gabriel shrank back into the car, waiting for Mr King to laugh. But he didn't. He stroked his long beard thoughtfully and smiled into the car.

'Funny you should say that. I often think the same thing, when I'm up in my glider. *Just like being an angel . . .*'

Suddenly, Gabriel didn't feel stupid any more. He sat up straight, and smiled back at Mr King. And his brothers leaned out of the car windows, calling out in loud, clear voices.

'Have you really got a glider?'

'Will you take us up in it?'

'Please!'

There was no more teasing that day. But Michael and Richard and Edward didn't forget. All the year, they roared with laughter if anyone mentioned angels. And when they were on the way to Grandmother's again, next Christmas, Michael pointed up at the sky.

'Hey, Gabe! After the carol service – when I've sung the solo – we might go up in Mr King's glider.'

'*Really?*' Gabriel's eyes glittered, and he bounced up and down in his seat. 'Me too?'

'Why don't you ask?' Michael said solemnly. 'Look, we're just going past the garage.'

Gabriel was so excited that he stuck his head out of the window. 'Mr King! Can *I* go in your glider?'

'What's that?' Mr King came forward, out of his little glass cabin. 'Say it again, lad.'

But Michael didn't give him a chance. He stuck his head out too. 'Gabriel wants a ride in your glider. He thinks he'll turn into an angel.'

Mr King didn't laugh, but Gabriel realized that it was just a tease. He went pink and pulled his head back into the car.

The next day, Michael sang the solo at the carol service, and all the old ladies muttered about what an angel he was. Gabriel shrank down into the pew. It felt just as if they were laughing at him.

That was Michael's last year as an angel. In June, his voice broke, and he couldn't do anything except growl and croak. When Christmas came, it was Richard who sang the solo. And two years after that, Edward had to take over.

It was a tradition in Grandmother's village. The first verse of the first carol had always been sung as a solo, by a child.

O come, all ye faithful,
Joyful and triumphant,
O come ye, O come ye
To Bethlehem . . .

But there were no children in the choir any more – hardly any children in the village, in fact. So, every year, one of Gabriel's brothers sang instead, with his fair hair gleaming and his blue eyes bright. And all the old men in the congregation smiled, and the old women dabbed at their eyes.

And Gabriel sat there wondering how Michael (or Richard or Edward) could be so brave. Singing in front of all those people.

Then, when Gabriel was eight, Edward's voice broke. One day, just before Christmas, he came down to breakfast and started singing, and everyone burst out laughing.

Gabriel laughed too – but not for long. Because Edward grinned at him.

'Looks like you'll be singing the solo this Christmas.'

'*Me?*' It came out in a strangled squeak.

'You!' Michael and Richard and Edward yelled. And they laughed even more. They thought he was fussing about nothing.

'It's easy,' Michael said. 'You just need a bit of practice.'

They stood Gabriel on a chair and Richard started humming, pretending to be the organ. 'Come on, now. Sing. *O come all ye faithful* . . .'

Gabriel tried. But the more he tried, the less noise he could make. When he looked round at the three of them, all staring, he felt as if he were choking to death. The only sound that would come out of his mouth was a strangled squeak.

'O *cme all ye fthfl . . .*'

The others burst out laughing and he jumped off the chair and ran upstairs. And after that, when anyone suggested practising, he looked away and mumbled that he'd done enough practising.

'Dne nff pracsing.'

Everyone believed him. And they were sure he would be all right. Why shouldn't he be? Singing was easy. Nobody knew how scared he was.

The nearer they got to Christmas, the worse it grew. When they were actually in the car, on the way to Grandmother's, he was so scared that he thought he was going to faint. He couldn't smile, even though his brothers tried all the old jokes.

'Look, Gabe. Angels up in the sky!'

'Mr King's going to give us a ride in one of those gliders.'

'After you've sung your solo.'

Gabriel turned away and stared out of the window. He knew he was running out of time. When they arrived at Grandmother's, he had to go straight to bed. And the next day it was the carol service.

The moment he opened his eyes, he thought, *I've got to practise. Before it's too late.* Maybe he would be all right if he found a place where no one could hear him.

He walked down to the far end of the garden and hid behind a rhododendron bush. But the moment he opened his mouth, he began to worry that someone would come. And he made the same strangled sounds as before. O *cme all ye fthful* . . .

He tried locking himself in the bathroom and turning on all the taps. But was the noise really loud enough to drown out his voice? Before he could make up his mind, Grandmother banged on the door to ask him why he was wasting all that water.

He tried putting his head under the bedclothes, with all the pillows heaped on top. But that just made him suffocate, so that he gasped and panted. *O-ho c-h-me all ye f-h-thf-h-l* . . .

And then it was lunchtime. And he'd just picked up his knife and fork when Grandmother said, 'All ready for the rehearsal then, Gabriel?'

'Rehearsal?' Gabriel stared.

Michael grinned. 'Gabriel doesn't need a rehearsal.'

'Nonsense!' Grandmother said briskly. 'You all went to the rehearsal. That's why you sang so well. Gabriel must rehearse too. I'll take him down to church as soon as we've washed up.'

Gabriel had forgotten about the rehearsal. He'd hardly noticed last year, when Edward slipped off to church in the afternoon. But he remembered now, and he knew he couldn't do it.

He couldn't walk into the church with Grandmother, and stand in front of all those men and women in the choir and sing O *cme all ye fthfl* . . . He couldn't.

He would have to run away.

He didn't manage to eat much lunch, but everyone just smiled and said he was excited. Then they all went off to the kitchen to wash up in Double Quick Time. Grandmother liked everything done in Double Quick Time. Gabriel waited until they were laughing and talking and teasing each other. Then he opened the front door and slipped out.

There were only two ways to go – left and right. The road to the left went up to the church, so he turned the other way, automatically. He went downhill, towards the garage, running as fast as he could, to get out of sight before anyone saw him.

He ran too fast. As he passed the garage, he caught his foot on a loose stone and went tumbling over, scraping his knees along the ground and banging his head on the Tarmac.

For a moment he just lay there, thinking that things were as bad as they could possibly be. Then he remembered that they would be even worse if anyone caught him, because he'd have to go to the rehearsal. He groaned and started dragging himself up.

But he was too late. Mr King had seen him fall over. He came out of the little glass office behind the petrol pumps and inspected Gabriel's knees.

'Nasty fall,' he said calmly. 'Come in and have a barley sugar.'

For a moment, Gabriel thought of running away. Then he realized that Mr King might run after him. He followed him into the glass cabin, limping a bit.

Mr King unhooked a bag of barley sugars from the display, opened it and gave one to Gabriel. Then he said, 'What are you doing down here this afternoon? I thought you'd be up at the church. Rehearsing.'

That was the last straw. Before he could stop himself, Gabriel burst into tears.

Mr King pulled a handkerchief out of his pocket and unfolded it. He watched Gabriel wipe his eyes and then said, 'What's up?'

'Gt t sng n the crl svice,' mumbled Gabriel, with his face in his hands. 'Nd m scared –'

'No use talking like that,' Mr King said. 'You know I can't hear. Take your hands away from your mouth and let me lip-read.'

Gabriel had forgotten Mr King was deaf. Dropping his hands, he made himself speak clearly. He was concentrating so hard on making the shapes of the words with his lips, that he didn't worry about what he was saying.

'I've got to sing the solo at the carol service. And I'm scared.'

Mr King nodded. 'Not surprised. There's only one way to get over that. Practice.'

Gabriel hung his head. 'Bt –' Then he remembered about Mr King's deafness, and he started again. 'But if I practise, the others laugh at me.'

'So you can't sing? In case they laugh?'

Gabriel nodded.

Mr King gave him another barley sugar and walked up and down for a bit. Then he stopped and looked at Gabriel.

'Want to come up in a glider?'

'Me?' Gabriel was so amazed that he didn't mumble at all. Mr King had never offered any of the others a flight. Even though they'd begged him, for years and years. 'Just me?'

'Just you,' Mr King said. 'Come on.'

They walked out of the cabin and he locked it behind them. Then he turned the big sign at the front of the forecourt, so that it said CLOSED instead of OPEN.

'We've just got time before it's too dark. If we hurry.'

They climbed into his Land Rover and it started with a judder and bounced down the hill towards Mr King's house. When they got there, Mr King put on the brake, very noisily, and said something.

Gabriel couldn't hear at first, because of the engine. Then he remembered about lip-reading and he saw what Mr King was saying. *Wait there while I fetch my brothers.*

There were two brothers. They both had beards, but one was fat and one was thin. They smiled as they climbed into the back of the Land Rover. With a crash of gears, Mr King drove out of the village and up to the glider field.

Gabriel had been to the field dozens of times. Whenever they came to the village, his brothers walked up there and stared longingly at the hangar where Mr King kept his red and white glider. If he was there, Mr King would smile and wave to them, but he never asked them into the field.

This time, he drove straight in and round the track at the edge of the field.

'Stay in the Land Rover,' he said to Gabriel.

Gabriel knew what was going to happen, because he'd seen it before. He watched Mr King's brothers open the hangar and wheel out the glider. He watched Mr King prepare the winch, and unwind the long cable that would pull the glider into the air.

The brothers settled the glider at the far end of the field and left it there, with the sun gleaming on its red and white paint. Then they came back up to the hangar. The fat brother found a helmet.

'Scared?' he said, as he adjusted the straps round Gabriel's chin.

'No.' Gabriel didn't see how anyone could be scared about going up in a glider. How could you be afraid of something wonderful?

Climbing into the cockpit, he settled himself in the front seat, with Mr King behind him. His heart was thudding against his ribs, but he knew he wasn't scared. He was excited.

The thin brother held on to the glider's wing and the fat one went down the field, to start the winch. Suddenly, the glider was racing forward, pulled by the cable. The thin brother ran along beside, holding it level.

'Here we go!' said Mr King.

And the glider took off.

It went up like a bird. Like an arrow shot from a bow. Rising into the air like something speeding up a steep, steep hill. Gabriel felt himself being pushed against the back of his seat. Up and up and up . . .

And then they stopped climbing.

'Look over the side,' Mr King's voice said, from behind.

Gabriel turned his head and saw the winch cable falling away as the glider levelled out. The cable had done its work and pulled them up, just as the string pulls a kite. Now they were in the sky, floating free. Riding the currents of the air.

It was very quiet. The only sounds Gabriel could hear were the creak of the wooden wings and the hiss of air round his head. He was sitting high in the sky, with nothing to shut him in.

Far below, he could see the village. The church where the choir was singing. The cars racing round the bypass. A train in the distance. They were all too far away to hear.

For a few minutes, the glider circled slowly, and Gabriel stared round. He was amazed how clearly he could see everything, even though it was such a long way down. It was like looking at the whole world.

'Beautiful, isn't it?' Mr King said.

Gabriel nodded. There was no way of saying how beautiful it was.

Mr King gave a small, soft chuckle. 'Always makes me want to sing.'

'*Do* you sing?' Gabriel said. 'Up here on your own?'

There was another chuckle. 'No use talking. I can't lip-read from here. Can't hear a thing you're saying.'

For a second, Gabriel felt stupid.

And then he understood what Mr King was telling him. They were up there on their own, just the two of them. And Mr King was deaf. *So no one could possibly hear any singing. No one in the whole world!*

But – wasn't it ridiculous? Singing in a glider?

Gabriel looked over the side, at the grey church spire, and the glittering line of the brook, and the big hills stretching away into the distance. The lovely, sunlit world. No, singing wasn't ridiculous. It was the only sensible thing to do.

He opened his mouth.

O come all ye faithful,
Joyful and triumphant . . .

It felt wonderful. Like yelling hurrah. Like blowing a fanfare on a trumpet.

Like being an angel.

The white wings of the glider gleamed in the winter sunshine. There was a small green car driving round the bypass. Maybe there was a little boy inside. Looking up at the glider and thinking it was an angel. Gabriel took a deep breath and sang as loudly and sweetly as he could.

O come let us adore him,
O come let us adore him,
O come let us adore him,
Christ the Lord!

He was still singing as the glider circled lower over the field. He didn't even realize they were landing, until they bumped lightly on to the grass, and Mr King's brothers came running forward to help him out of his seat.

'That was a nice bit of singing,' said the thin brother.

'Look forward to hearing you in church,' said the fat brother.

Gabriel went pink and hung his head. 'Bt tht's diffrnt.'

Mr King tapped his shoulder. 'What did you say?'

Gabriel felt silly, but he turned round and spoke clearly. 'I said that's different. Singing in church.'

'Don't see why,' Mr King said. 'Shut your eyes, and you can be anywhere you like.'

The brothers both nodded, and Gabriel frowned. What did they mean?

'Time to go home,' Mr King said. 'I'll take you up. These two will put the glider away. Hop in the Land Rover, lad.'

As Gabriel climbed in, he suddenly wondered what he was going to say when he got back to Grandmother's house. She would be furious with him. How could he explain why he'd run away?

He didn't have to explain anything. When they reached the house, Mr King went in on his own, leaving Gabriel to wait in the Land Rover. When he came out again, Grandmother was with him. She was smiling.

'You've missed the rehearsal, but it sounds as though you don't need one. Mr King tells me you're a wonderful singer.'

'But –' *But Mr King can't hear . . .*

Grandmother didn't give Gabriel time to say it. She caught hold of his arm. 'Hurry up, or we'll be late for the service.'

Michael came bounding out of the house in his best clothes. 'Gabriel can't go to church like that. He's wearing jeans.'

'Don't be silly,' Grandmother said. 'And anyway, no one will see when he's got the choir robes on. Come along, Gabriel.'

She hustled him down the path, with the rest of the family scurrying behind. Michael ran to catch up, whispering in Gabriel's ear.

'Where have you been?'

'In a glider,' Gabriel said.

'Oh, ha ha!' Michael pulled a face. 'Stop teasing.'

Teasing? 'Mr King took me up.'

Richard jogged up. 'Don't be silly. The garage is open on Friday afternoons. Mr King must have been there.'

Gabriel couldn't answer, because they'd reached the church, and Grandmother was chivvying him round to the vestry. She buttoned him into a long blue cassock and slipped a white surplice over his head. Then she nodded approvingly.

'You look very nice. Even better than your brothers.'

Gabriel didn't care how he looked. As she pushed him into line with the rest of the choir, he was shaking. And when they walked into church, he nearly fainted. All the front pews were full. People were going to *hear* him. He couldn't sing. He *couldn't*.

The organist began the introduction to the first carol. Gabriel felt his throat go dry. He knew he wouldn't be able to make any sound except a squeak. He knew it. But there was no escape.

He opened his mouth.

And then, at the last moment, he saw Mr King, sitting at the back of the church, looking at him. Slowly and deliberately, Mr King closed his eyes. *Shut your eyes, and you can be anywhere you like.*

All at once, Gabriel understood. He closed his own eyes – and he wasn't looking at rows of people any more. He was in the glider, circling like an angel. The sunshine was glittering on the snow-white wings, and the beautiful world was spread out below.

He started to sing, as sweetly as he could.

O come all ye faithful . . .

He didn't open his eyes until the whole carol was over. When he did, he saw his brothers, sitting in the front pew, staring at him. Wondering whether it could be possibly true about the glider. He almost burst out laughing.

But he didn't laugh. He stared straight ahead, looking solemn and good, and he heard the old ladies whispering to each other.

'Just like an angel . . .'

I'll do it even better next year, he thought. And he started smiling. He had years and years left before his voice broke. Years and years of being a Christmas angel.

Why the Chimes Rang

RAYMOND MACDONALD ALDEN

THERE WAS once, in a faraway country where few people have ever travelled, a wonderful church. It stood on a high hill in the midst of a great city; and every Sunday, as well as on sacred days like Christmas, thousands of people climbed the hill to its great archways, looking like lines of ants all moving in the same direction.

When you came to the building itself, you found stone columns and dark passages, and a grand entrance leading to a main room of the church.

This room was so long that one standing at the doorway could scarcely see to the other end, where the choir stood by the marble altar. In the farthest corner was the organ; and this organ was so loud that, sometimes when it played, the people for miles around would close their shutters and prepare for a great thunderstorm. Altogether, no such church as this was ever seen before, especially when it was lighted up for some festival, and crowded with people, young and old. But the strangest thing about the whole building was the wonderful chime of bells.

At one corner of the church was a great grey tower, with ivy growing over it as far up as one could see. I say as far as one could see, because the tower was quite great enough to fit the great church, and it rose so far into the sky that it was only in very fair weather that anyone claimed to be able to see the top.

Even then one could not be certain that it was in sight. Up, and up, and up climbed the stones and the ivy; and, as the men who built the church had been dead for hundreds of years, everyone had forgotten how high the tower was supposed to be.

Now all the people knew that at the top of the tower was a chime of Christmas bells. They had hung there ever since the church had been built, and were the most beautiful bells in the world. Some thought it was because a great musician had cast them and arranged them in their place; others said it was because of the great height, which reached up where the air was clearest and purest; however that might be, no one who had ever heard the chimes denied that they were the sweetest in the world. Some described them as sounding like angels far up in the sky; others, as sounding like strange winds singing throughout the trees.

But the fact was that no one had heard them for years and years. There was an old man living not far from the church, who said that his mother had spoken of hearing them when she was a little girl, and he was the only one who was sure of as much as that. They were Christmas chimes, you see, and were not meant to be played by men or on common days. It was the custom on Christmas Eve for all the people to bring to the church their offerings to the Christ Child; and when the greatest and best offering was laid on the altar, there used to come sounding through the music of the choir the Christmas chimes far up in the tower. Some said that the wind rang them, and others that they were so high that the angels could set them swinging. But for many long years they had never been heard. It was said that people had been growing less careful of their gifts for the Christ Child, and that no offering was brought great enough to deserve the music of the chimes.

Every Christmas Eve the rich people still crowded to the altar, each one trying to bring some better gift than any other, without giving anything that he wanted for himself, and the church was crowded with those who thought that perhaps the wonderful bells might be heard again. But although the service was splendid, and the offerings plenty, only the roar of the wind could be heard, far up in the stone tower.

Now, a number of miles from the city, in a little country village, where nothing could be seen of the great church but glimpses of the tower when the weather was fine, lived a boy named Pedro, and his little brother. They knew very little about the Christmas chimes, but they had heard of the service in the church on Christmas Eve, and had a secret plan, which they had often talked over when by themselves, to go to see the beautiful celebration.

'Nobody can guess, Little Brother,' Pedro would say, 'all the fine things there are to see and hear; and I have even heard it said that the Christ Child sometimes comes down to bless the service. What if we could see Him?'

The day before Christmas was bitterly cold, with a few lonely snowflakes flying in the air, and a hard white crust on the ground. Sure enough, Pedro and Little Brother were able to slip quietly away early in the afternoon; and although the walking was hard in the frosty air, before nightfall they had trudged so far, hand in hand, that they saw the lights of the big city just ahead of them. Indeed, they were about to enter one of the great gates in the wall that surrounded it, when they saw something dark on the snow near their path, and stepped aside to look at it.

It was a poor woman, who had fallen just outside the city, too sick and tired to get in where she might have found shelter. The soft snow made of a drift a sort of pillow for her, and she would soon be so sound asleep, in the wintry air, that no one could ever waken her again.

All this Pedro saw in a moment, and he knelt down beside her and tried to rouse her, even tugging at her arm a little, as though he would have tried to carry her away. He turned her face towards him, so that he could rub some of the snow on it, and when he had looked at her silently a moment he stood up again, and said:

'It's no use, Little Brother. You will have to go on alone.'

'Alone?' cried Little Brother. 'And you not see the Christmas festival?'

'No,' said Pedro, and he could not keep back a bit of a choking sound in his throat. 'See this poor woman. Her face looks like the Madonna in the chapel window, and she will freeze to death if nobody cares for her. Everyone has gone to the church now, but when you come back you can bring someone to help her. I will rub her to keep her from freezing, and perhaps get her to eat the bun that is left in my pocket.'

'But I cannot bear to leave you, and go on alone,' said Little Brother.

'Both of us need not miss the service,' said Pedro, 'and it had better be I than you. You can easily find your way to the church; and you must see and hear everything twice, Little Brother – once for you and once for me. I am sure the Christ Child must know how I should love to come with you and worship Him; and oh! if you get a chance, Little Brother, to slip up to the altar without getting in anyone's way, take this little silver piece of mine, and lay it down for my offering, when no one is looking. Do not forget where you have left me, and forgive me for not going with you.'

In this way he hurried Little Brother off to the city, and winked hard to keep back the tears, as he heard the crunching footsteps sounding farther and farther away in the twilight. It was pretty hard to lose the music and splendour of the Christmas celebration that he had been planning for so long, and spend the time instead in that lonely place in the snow.

The great church was a wonderful place that night. Everyone said that it had never looked so bright and beautiful before. When the organ played and the thousands of people sang, the walls shook with the sound, and little Pedro, away outside the city wall, felt the earth tremble around him.

At the close of the service came the procession with the offerings to be laid on the altar. Rich men and great men marched proudly up to lay down their gifts to the Christ Child. Some brought wonderful jewels, some baskets of gold so heavy that they could scarcely carry them down the aisle. A great writer laid down a book that he had been making for years and years. And last of all walked the king of the country, hoping with all the rest to win for himself the chime of the Christmas bells. There went a great murmur throughout the church, as the people saw the king take from his head the royal crown, all set with precious stones, and lay it gleaming on the altar, as his offering to the Holy Child. 'Surely,' everyone said, 'we shall hear the bells now, for nothing like this has ever happened before.'

But still only the cold old wind was heard in the tower, and the people shook their heads; and some of them said, as they had before, that they never really believed the story of the chimes, and doubted if they ever rang at all.

The procession was over, and the choir began the closing hymn. Suddenly the organist stopped playing as though he had been shot, and everyone looked at the old minister, who was standing by the altar, holding up his hand for silence. Not a sound could be heard from anyone in the church, but as all the people strained their ears to listen, there came softly, but distinctly, swinging through the air, the sound of the chimes in the tower. So far away, and yet so clear the music seemed – so much sweeter were the notes than anything that had been heard before, rising and falling away up there in the sky, that the people in the church sat for a moment as still as though something held each of them by the shoulders. Then they all stood up together and stared straight at the altar, to see what great gift had awakened the long-silent bells.

But all that the nearest of them saw was the childish figure of Little Brother, who had crept softly down the aisle when no one was looking, and had laid Pedro's little piece of silver on the altar.

The Box of Magic

MALORIE BLACKMAN

IT WAS Christmas Eve, but Peter was in no hurry. His head bent, Peter dragged his feet as he made his way slowly home. There was no point in rushing. Mum and Dad would only be arguing about something or another. Peter and his sister Chloe had hoped that the quarrelling would stop over Christmas. It hadn't. If anything, it'd got worse.

Peter had spent all afternoon searching and searching for the perfect present for his mum and dad. Something that would stop them quarrelling for just five minutes. Something that would make

Christmas the way it used to be, with smiles and songs and happiness in every corner of the house. But all the searching had been for nothing. Peter didn't have that much money to begin with and all the things he could afford, he didn't want. All the gifts he could afford looked so cheap and tacky that Peter knew they would fall apart about ten seconds after they were handled. What was he going to do? He had to buy something and time was running out.

Then he caught sight of it out of the corner of his eye.

The medium-sized sign above the door said 'THE CHRISTMAS SHOP' in spidery writing. The small shop window was framed with silver and gold tinsel and a scattering of glitter like mini stars. At the bottom of the window, fake snow had been sprayed. It looked so much like the real thing that had it been outside the window instead of inside, Peter would've been sure it was real snow. A single Christmas tree, laden down with fairy lights and baubles and yet more tinsel, stood proudly in the exact centre of the window.

Peter stood in front of the shop and stared. He'd never seen anything so . . . wonderful! It was as if Christmas had started in this shop and then spread out to cover the whole wide world.

'The Christmas Shop . . .' Peter muttered to himself.

He wondered why he'd never seen it before. True, it was behind the shopping precinct and he usually walked through the precinct not around it, but even so. Peter looked up and down the street. The few other shops in the same row as the Christmas Shop were all boarded up.

Unexpectedly, the shop door opened. A tall portly man with a white beard and a merry twinkle in his eyes stood in the doorway.

'Hello! Come in! Come in!' The shopkeeper beckoned.

'I . . . er . . . don't have much money.' Peter shook his head.

'No matter. Come in.' The shopkeeper turned and held the door open. It was as if there was no doubt in his mind that Peter would enter. Uncertainly, Peter dithered on the pavement. He hadn't intended to go in. He was only window shopping. But the shop looked so warm and inviting and the shopkeeper seemed so friendly. Peter walked into the shop.

And he gasped in amazement!

It was even better inside than it had appeared from outside. It smelt of freshly baked bread and warm cakes and toast and cinnamon and nutmeg and it was so warm, it was as if the sun itself had come for a visit.

'Isn't my shop the best!' smiled the shopkeeper. 'Look around. Feel free. You can pick up anything, touch anything.'

Peter stared at the shopkeeper. He certainly wasn't like any other shopkeeper Peter had ever met. Usually shopkeepers didn't like school kids in their shops and they certainly didn't like them touching things. Peter wandered around the shop, his dark brown eyes wide with delight. Toys and games and Christmas sweets and Christmas treats filled every corner.

Peter's hand curled around the money in his pocket. He could buy all his Christmas presents in here. Peter bent his head to examine a gold and berry-red scarf. That would be perfect for his mum. And maybe the night-blue and yellow scarf for his dad. And he could get that little glass unicorn over there for Chloe. That was just the kind of thing she liked. The strange thing was, none of the items had prices on them.

'H-How much are these woolly scarves?' Peter asked, crossing his fingers in his pockets. 'And how much is that unicorn over there?'

'That depends on who they're for and why you think they'd like them,' answered the shopkeeper.

'The scarves are for my mum and dad and the unicorn is for my sister. Chloe likes things made of glass. She keeps them in her bedroom on the windowsill. And I thought that Mum and Dad could have the scarves to keep them warm.'

'And how much money do you have?' asked the shopkeeper.

Peter took out all the money in his pocket. The shopkeeper checked through it carefully.

'You're lucky,' said the shopkeeper. 'You've got enough for all the things you want.'

'I have? Really?' Peter couldn't believe it.

The shopkeeper smiled and nodded. Peter grinned at him, but slowly his smile faded. He'd buy the scarves for his dad and mum and then what? What good would any present do? Peter could see it now. Mum and Dad opening their presents on Christmas Day.

'Thanks, Peter. That's great,' says Dad.

'Peter, that's wonderful,' says Mum.

And then they'd fling their presents to the back of the chair and start shouting at each other again.

'What's the matter, Peter?' asked the shopkeeper gently.

Peter jumped. He'd been lost in a world of his own.

'It's just that . . . Hang on a second. How did you know my name?' Peter stared.

'It's a little game of mine,' the shopkeeper beamed. 'I like to guess people's names, and nine times out of ten, I get it right.'

Peter was impressed.

'So you were saying?' the shopkeeper prompted.

'I . . . I don't suppose you've got anything in your shop to stop my mum and dad from fighting?' The moment the words were out of his mouth, Peter regretted it. What was he doing? He hadn't told anyone about his mum and dad, not even his best friend Andy. No one knew how things were at home except his sister Chloe, and she didn't talk about it either.

'Oh, I see. Do your mum and dad argue a lot?' asked the shopkeeper.

'All the time,' Peter sighed.

The shopkeeper pursed his lips. 'Hhmm! I think I have just the present you need – for your whole family.'

The shopkeeper went around his brightly coloured counter and disappeared down behind it. Moments later he straightened up, a huge smile on his face and a silver box in his hands.

'These are what you need,' he said.

'What are they?' Peter asked doubtfully.

'Christmas crackers,' announced the shopkeeper proudly. At the disappointed look on Peter's face, he added, 'Ah, but they're not just any crackers. They're magic. Guaranteed to work or your money back.'

'How are they magic?' Peter asked suspiciously.

'The magic only works if they're pulled on Christmas Day, when you're all around the table eating dinner,' explained the shopkeeper.

'But how do they work?'

'It's hard to explain. You have to see the magic for yourself.'

'How much are they?' asked Peter, still doubtful. Maybe he could buy them and still get the other presents as well.

'I'm afraid they're very expensive because they're magic,' said the shopkeeper. 'They'll cost you all the money you've got, and even then I'm letting you have them cheap.'

Peter thought for a moment. Magic crackers. Crackers that would actually stop Mum and Dad from arguing. They were worth the money if they could do that. He took a deep breath.

'All right, I'll take them,' he said quickly, before he could change his mind.

Peter handed over his money and the shopkeeper handed over the box of eight crackers. Moments later, Peter was out of the shop and running all the way home. Magic crackers! He couldn't wait for Christmas Day.

'I've been in that kitchen since seven o'clock this morning. I think the least you could do is sit at the table with the rest of your family.' Mum's voice dripped with ice.

'I want to watch the end of this film,' Dad argued.

'Typical! You're so selfish,' Mum snapped.

Peter and Chloe looked at each other and sighed. Mum and Dad were at it again. Christmas Day – and they were still arguing.

'Dad, you and Mum and Chloe can open my present now,' Peter said desperately. 'The man in the Christmas Shop said they should only be opened when we're all sitting round the table eating dinner.'

'Oh, all right then,' Dad grumbled.

'Oh, I see. You'll come to the table if Peter asks you to, but not if I ask you,' sniffed Mum.

'Peter doesn't nag me every two seconds,' Dad said as he sat down at the table.

Chloe shook her head and turned to look out of the window. Peter ran to get the present he'd bought. It was the only one left unopened under the tree. He stood between his mum and dad, putting the present down on the tablecloth. Mum and Dad looked at each other.

'Go on then,' Dad prompted.

'You do it,' said Mum.

'I'll do it,' said Chloe.

She tore off the bright red and yellow wrapping paper.

'It's a box of crackers,' she said, surprised.

'Not just any crackers,' Peter said eagerly. 'They're *magic* crackers!'

'Who told you that?' Mum smiled.

'The man in the Christmas Shop,' Peter replied.

'Well, let's all sit down. Then we can pull them and get on with our dinner,' said Dad, adding under his breath, 'And maybe then I can get back to my film.'

But the moment they all sat down, something peculiar began to happen. A strange feeling settled over the dinner table. A hopeful, expectant feeling – as if, in spite of themselves, everyone was waiting for something terrific, amazing *and* spectacular to happen all at once. The noise from the telly was just a distant hum at the other end of the room. Light, like warm spring sunshine, came from everyone, smiling at everyone else as they watched Dad place two crackers beside each plate. Chloe held out her cracker to Dad. Peter held his Christmas cracker out to Mum.

'One! Two! Three!' they all shouted.

Bang! Pop! The sound of exploding crackers filled the room. Chloe and Peter got the biggest parts of the crackers. They both peered down into them.

'They're . . . they're *empty*!' Chloe exclaimed.

'No! They can't be,' frowned Mum.

'See for yourself,' said Chloe, handing over her cracker.

Peter couldn't believe it. Empty . . . When he remembered the smiling, friendly face of the jolly man with the white beard in the Christmas Shop, he just *couldn't* believe it. That man wouldn't take his money and sell him a box of *nothing* – Peter was sure he wouldn't. And yet . . . and yet, his cracker was empty. Just an empty roll covered with some glossy paper and nothing else. No hats. No jokes. No gifts. Nothing.

'Maybe there were just two duff ones in the box,' Mum suggested.

Mum and Dad pulled their crackers next. The same thing happened. They were empty. Chloe and Peter pulled crackers five and six at the same time as Mum and Dad pulled crackers seven and eight.

They were all empty.

Peter examined each one, hoping against hope that they'd got it wrong or it was a trick – but it wasn't. Peter looked at Chloe, then Mum and Dad – and burst into tears. He couldn't help it.

'The shopkeeper told me they were magic crackers,' Peter sobbed to Mum and Dad. 'I only bought them because he said they would make you stop arguing with each other. He promised me they were magic. He *promised* me . . .'

Dad stared. Mum's mouth fell open.

'You . . . you bought them – because of *us*?' Dad asked, aghast.

Peter sniffed and nodded.

'Never mind, Peter.' Chloe put her arm around her younger brother's shoulder. 'Besides, nothing would stop Mum and Dad from fighting. Not even a real box of magic crackers.' And with that, Chloe burst into tears too.

'Chloe! Peter!' Mum and Dad ran around the table to hug Peter and Chloe to them. 'We had no idea we were quarrelling that much.'

'And we had no idea we were upsetting both of you so much,' said Dad.

But Peter and Chloe couldn't stop crying.

'I'll tell you what,' said Mum. 'Let's make our own Christmas crackers. All this food will stay warm in the oven until we've finished.'

'Terrific idea.' Dad went over to the telly and switched it off. 'We'll make the hats first,' Dad continued. 'Out of newspaper.'

Dad and Mum showed Peter and Chloe how to make sailor hats out of newspaper. That took about five minutes. Then they all sat down for dinner. Over dinner, everyone had to tell the worst jokes they knew, like, 'How do you make an apple puff? Chase it round the garden!' and 'Why did the elephant cross the road? Because it was the chicken's day off!' Dad's joke was 'Why did silly Billy stand on a ladder when he was learning to sing? So he could reach the high notes!' And Mum's joke was ancient but she was still proud of it! 'How do you make a Swiss Roll? Push him down a hill!' Chloe told a joke that Peter didn't get until Mum explained it. 'How do you tell how old a telephone is? Count its rings!' (Mum explained that you could tell the age of a tree by counting the rings through its trunk.) Everyone got Peter's joke. 'Why are vampires crazy? Because they're often bats!' And when anyone ran out of jokes, they made them up, which was even funnier!

After dinner when everyone was eating Christmas pudding, Mum grabbed Dad and whispered in his ear. Suddenly they both dashed off upstairs with the empty crackers. Ten minutes later they reappeared with the various ends of each cracker now glued together.

'Cracker time!' said Mum. And she held out a cracker to Chloe.

They both pulled.

'POP!' shouted Mum.

Chloe looked inside the cracker and there was one of Mum's old bangles – the gold and blue one which had always been Chloe's favourite.

'Your turn,' said Dad, holding out a cracker to Peter. They both shouted, 'BANG!'

Peter looked inside the cracker. There was a pig made of lego bricks. At least, that's what Peter thought it was.

'It's not a pig. It's a rocket!' said Dad indignantly.

Mum started to giggle. 'I told you it looked more like a pig, dear,' she said.

They 'popped' the rest of the crackers. They all had very silly, very tacky, very wonderful presents in them.

'Who needs rotten, mouldy old crackers?' asked Dad. 'We can do it all ourselves.'

'And they're much better too,' Mum agreed. 'It's just a shame that Peter got conned out of his money. Where did you say the shop was?'

'Behind the precinct. All the other shops on the same street were boarded up,' Peter replied.

'There aren't any shops behind the precinct. The last one closed down over a year ago,' Dad frowned.

'There's one still open. It's called the Christmas Shop,' said Peter.

Mum and Dad looked at each other. They both shrugged.

'Never mind. I'd say they were the best crackers we've ever had,' smiled Mum. 'My jaw still aches from laughing at all those terrible jokes.'

'Those crackers were . . . a box of magic,' said Dad, giving Mum a cuddle.

Later that night, as Peter lay in bed, he still couldn't quite believe what had happened. Mum and Dad hadn't argued once since the crackers had been pulled. In fact, it was the most wonderful day they'd all had in a long, long time. The only cloud was the shopkeeper who'd sold Peter the crackers in the first place. Peter still didn't want to believe that the shopkeeper was a crook who had deliberately diddled him out of his money.

A strange tinkling-clinking came from across the room, followed by a plopping sound. Peter sat up and frowned. What was that? He switched on his bedside light. There it was again – the same strange noise. And it seemed to be coming from his chair over by the window. Over the back of the chair were the jumper and the pair of trousers Peter had worn on Christmas Eve. That strange noise couldn't be coming from them – could it? Swallowing hard, Peter got up and tiptoed across to the chair.

Tinkle! Clinkle! Plop!

There it was again! Peter took a deep breath, counted to three, then quickly pulled the chair to one side. More money fell out of his trouser pockets and plopped on to the carpet. Peter's eyes goggled! Where had all that money come from? He scooped up the money on the floor, then picked up his trousers and dug into his pockets. There was more money inside them. He counted it all very carefully. It was the exact amount of money he had paid for the Christmas crackers . . .

Peter sat down on his bed and stared down at the money in his hand. What was going on? He shook his head and looked around the room hoping for some clue. Had Mum and Dad done it? Had they put the money in his pockets to make up for him losing his money in the Christmas Shop? But they didn't know exactly how much he'd paid for the crackers. And now here he was, with the exact same coins in his hand.

Then something else caught his eye. There on his bedside table, were all the Christmas cards he'd received from his friends. At the front was the card he'd got from his best friend Andy. Peter gasped and stared so hard, his eyes began to ache.

The face on the card . . .

Peter had seen that face before – in the Christmas Shop. The shopkeeper and Father Christmas were one and the same person . . . Peter picked up the card and studied it. The shopkeeper *was* Father Christmas. Peter was sure of it. And that would explain how he'd got his money back. Which meant only one thing . . .

The Christmas crackers *were* magic after all.

'Thank you,' Peter whispered to the Christmas card.

And he was sure that on the card, the smiling face of Father Christmas winked at him.

Christmas Is Coming

from *The Country Child*, set in 1931

ALISON UTTLEY

AT CHRISTMAS the wind ceased to moan. Snow lay thick on the fields and the woods cast blue shadows across it. The fir trees were like sparkling, gem-laden Christmas trees, the only ones Susan had ever seen. The orchard, with the lacy old boughs outlined with snow, was a grove of fairy trees. The woods were enchanted, exquisite, the trees were holy, and anything harmful had shrunken to a thin wisp and had retreated into the depths.

The fields lay with their unevennesses gone and paths obliterated, smooth white slopes criss-crossed by black lines running up to the woods. More than ever the farm seemed under a spell, like a toy in the forest, with little wooden animals and men; a brown horse led by a stiff little red-scarfed man to a yellow stable door; round, white, woolly sheep clustering round a blue trough of orange mangolds; red cows drinking from a square, white trough, and returning to a painted cow-house.

Footprints were everywhere on the snow, rabbits and foxes, blackbirds, pheasants and partridges, trails of small paws, the mark of a brush, and the long feet of the cock pheasant and the tip-mark of his tail.

A jay flew out of the wood like a blue flashing diamond and came to the grass-plot for bread. A robin entered the house and hopped under the table while Susan sat very still and her father sprinkled crumbs on the floor.

Rats crouched outside the window, peeping out of the walls with gleaming eyes, seizing the birds' crumbs and scraps, and slowly lolloping back again.

Red squirrels ran along the walls to the back door, close to the window, to eat the crumbs on the bench where the milk cans froze. Every wild animal felt that a truce had come with the snow, and they visited the house where there was food in plenty, and sat with paws uplifted and noses twitching.

For the granaries were full, it had been a prosperous year, and there was food for everyone. Not like the year before when there was so little hay that Mr Garland had to buy a stack in February. Three large haystacks as big as houses stood in the stackyard, thatched evenly and straight by Job Fletcher, who was the best thatcher for many a mile. Great mounds showed where the roots were buried. The brick-lined pit was filled with grains and in the barns were stores of corn.

The old brew-house was full of logs of wood, piled high against the walls, cut from trees which the wind had blown down. The coal-house with its strong ivied walls, part of the old fortress, had been stored with coal brought many a mile in the blaze of summer; twenty tons lay under the snow.

On the kitchen walls hung the sides of bacon and from hooks in the ceiling dangled great hams and shoulders. Bunches of onions were twisted in the pantry and barn, and an empty cow-house was stored with potatoes for immediate use.

The floor of the apple chamber was covered with apples, rosy apples, little yellow ones, like cowslip balls, wizenedy apples with withered, wrinkled cheeks, fat, well-fed smooth-faced apples, and immense green cookers, pointed like a house, which would burst in the oven and pour out a thick cream of the very essence of apples.

Even the cheese chamber had its cheeses this year, for there had been too much milk for the milkman, and the cheese presses had been put into use again. Some of them were Christmas cheese, with layers of sage running through the middles like green ribbons.

Stone jars like those in which the forty thieves hid stood on the pantry floor, filled with white lard, and balls of fat tied up in bladders hung from the hooks. Along the broad shelves round the walls were pots of jam, blackberry and apple, from the woods and orchard, Victoria plum from the trees on house and barn, blackcurrant from the garden, and redcurrant jelly, damson cheese from the half-wild ancient trees which grew everywhere, leaning over walls, dropping their blue fruit on paths and walls, in pigsty and orchard, in field and water trough, so that Susan thought they were wild as hips and haws.

Pickles and spices filled old brown pots decorated with crosses and flowers, like the pitchers and crocks of Will Shakespeare's time.

In the little dark wine chamber under the stairs were bottles of elderberry wine, purple, thick, and sweet, and golden cowslip wine, and hot ginger, some of them many years old, waiting for the winter festivities.

There were dishes piled with mince pies on the shelves of the larder, and a row of plum puddings with their white calico caps, and strings of sausages, and round pats of butter, with swans and cows and wheat-ears printed upon them.

Everyone who called at the farm had to eat and drink at Christmas-tide.

A few days before Christmas, Mr Garland and Dan took a bill-hook and knife and went into the woods to cut branches of scarlet-berried holly. They tied them together with ropes and dragged them down over the fields to the barn. Mr Garland cut a bough of mistletoe from the ancient hollow hawthorn which leaned over the wall by the orchard, and thick clumps of dark-berried ivy from the walls.

Indoors, Mrs Garland and Susan and Becky polished and rubbed and cleaned the furniture and brasses, so that everything glowed and glittered. They decorated every room, from the kitchen where every lustre jug had its sprig in its mouth, every brass candlestick had its chaplet, every copper saucepan and preserving-pan had its wreath of shining berries and leaves, through the hall, which was a bower of green, to the two parlours which were festooned and hung with holly and boughs of fir, and ivy berries dipped in red raddle, left over from sheep marking.

Holly decked every picture and ornament. Sprays hung over the bacon and twisted round the hams and herb bunches. The clock carried a crown on his head, and every dish-cover had a little sprig. Susan kept an eye on the lonely forgotten humble things, the jelly moulds and colanders and nutmeg-grater, and made them happy with glossy leaves. Everything seemed to speak, to ask for its morsel of greenery, and she tried to leave out nothing.

On Christmas Eve fires blazed in the kitchen and parlour and even in the bedrooms. Becky ran from room to room with the red-hot salamander which she stuck between the bars to make a blaze, and Mrs Garland took the copper warming-pan filled with glowing cinders from the kitchen fire and rubbed it between the sheets of all the beds. Susan had come down to her cosy tiny room with thick curtains at the window, and a fire in the big fireplace. Flames roared up the chimneys as Dan carried in the logs and Becky piled them on the blaze. The wind came back and tried to get in, howling at the key holes, but all the shutters were cottered and the doors shut. The horses and mares stood in the stables, warm and happy, with nodding heads. The cows slept in the cow-houses, the sheep in the open sheds. Only Rover stood at the door of his kennel, staring up at the sky, howling to the dog in the moon, and then he too turned and lay down in his straw.

In the middle of the kitchen ceiling there hung the kissing-bunch, the best and brightest pieces of holly made in the shape of a large ball, which dangled from the hook. Silver and gilt drops, crimson bells, blue glass trumpets, bright oranges and red polished apples, peeped and glittered through the glossy leaves. Little flags of all nations, but chiefly Turkish for some unknown reason, stuck out like quills on a hedgehog. The lamp hung near, and every little berry, every leaf, every pretty ball and apple had a tiny yellow flame reflected in its heart.

Twisted candles hung down, yellow, red, and blue, unlighted but gay, and on either side was a string of paper lanterns.

Mrs Garland climbed on a stool and nailed on the wall the Christmas texts, 'God bless our Home', 'God is Love', 'Peace be on this House', 'A Happy Christmas and a Bright New Year'.

So the preparations were made. Susan hung up her stocking at the foot of the bed and fell asleep. But soon singing roused her and she sat, bewildered. Yes, it was the carol singers.

Outside under the stars she could see the group of men and women, with lanterns throwing beams across the paths and on to the stable door. One man stood apart beating time, another played a fiddle and another had a flute. The rest sang in four parts the Christmas hymns, 'While Shepherds Watched', 'O Come, all Ye faithful', and 'Hark the Herald Angels Sing'.

There was the Star, Susan could see it twinkling and bright in the dark boughs with their white frosted layers; and there was the stable. She watched the faces half-lit by lanterns. A bright light flickered across the snow as the door was flung wide open. Then a bang, and Susan went back to bed. Christmas Eve was nearly over, but tomorrow was Christmas Day, the best day in all the year.

The Story of the Christmas Rose

inspired by a Scandinavian legend

RETOLD BY NORAH MONTGOMERIE

LONG, LONG ago there was a Robber family who lived in the Great Forest. Robber Father had stolen sheep and the Bishop had made him an outlaw. So the Robber family went into the forest and there they lived in the shelter of a deep cave, for they had nowhere else to go. Robber Father hunted for food, while Robber Mother and their five children gathered berries to eat, ferns for their beds and wood for the fire.

Sometimes Robber Mother took the children into the village to beg, but they looked so rough and wild with their unkempt hair and their ragged clothes, people were afraid of them and locked their doors when they saw them coming. Sometimes the people left a bundle of old clothes or a parcel of food outside the door for Robber Mother to collect. But not once did they ask her in or even say a word of greeting, as they did to any stranger. This made Robber Mother furious. She scowled and muttered to herself, even when her sack was full, and looked more fierce than ever.

One warm summer day, as she trudged home, her sack slung over her shoulder, Robber Mother saw that a little door in the monastery wall had been left open. She stopped and peeped in. There she saw a beautiful garden filled with bright flowers. Honeysuckle, red roses and white jasmine covered the grey stone walls, and she had never seen so many butterflies. She put down her sack and walked into the garden. She bent down to smell the pink roses and smiled.

You can imagine how surprised the monastery gardener was when he saw the rough Robber Mother in his beautiful garden.

'Hi there!' he shouted. 'You can't come in here, this is the Abbot's private garden. No women are allowed in here. Be off with you!'

Robber Mother looked up and scowled fiercely.

'I'm doing no harm,' she snapped, 'and I'll go when I've found what I'm looking for.'

'You'll go right now, my good woman,' shouted the gardener, 'or I'll throw you out!'

'Just you try!' laughed Robber Mother, who was much bigger than the gardener and probably stronger too.

This made the gardener very angry. He went off and fetched two fat monks who tried to put her out. But she bit and kicked and screamed, and made such a noise that the old Abbot came hurrying out to see what all the fuss was about.

'This woman won't leave your garden, Lord Abbot,' said one of the monks.

'Leave her to me, brothers, I will deal with her,' said the Abbot and turning to Robber Mother, he said, 'I expect you have never seen such a fine garden, my good woman. Do you want to pick some of the flowers?'

'I do not,' said Robber Mother. 'This is a fine garden, but it cannot compare with the one we have in the Great Forest every Christmas.'

'Is that so?' laughed the Abbot. His garden was his pride and joy and was said to be the finest in the land. But Robber Mother said angrily:

'I'm not joking, Lord Abbot, I know what I'm saying. Every Christmas Eve, part of the Great Forest near our cave is transformed into a wonderful garden to celebrate the birth of the Christ Child. We who live in the forest see it every year. In that garden flowers of all the seasons grow together at the same time, and there are flowers there I would not dare to touch, they are so beautiful. They have frail silver petals and pale gold stamens. We call them Christmas roses. I do not see them in your garden.'

The old Abbot listened to Robber Mother. He remembered hearing, as a child, how part of the Great Forest was transformed into a beautiful garden on Christmas Eve. He had longed to see it and then he had forgotten all about it. So he smiled kindly at Robber Mother.

'I have heard of your garden,' he said, 'and I would like to see it. Would you send one of your children to guide me to the spot next Christmas Eve?'

'How can we be sure you will not drive us away from our cave if we show you where it is?' said Robber Mother.

'I would not do that,' said the Abbot. 'I would rather ask my Lord Bishop to grant your husband a free pardon in return for your kindness.'

'You would do that?' asked Robber Mother eagerly.

'Yes, I shall ask,' said the old Abbot, 'but whether my Lord Bishop will grant my request I do not know.'

'I trust you,' said Robber Mother, 'and my eldest boy will wait for you next Christmas Eve and guide you through the Great Forest to our cave. He will wait for you by the old oak. But you must promise you will bring only one companion with you – this gardener here.'

'I promise,' said the Abbot, and after he had blessed the Robber Mother, she left the garden quietly and returned home.

The Abbot went to the Bishop and told him all that had happened, and the story of the Christmas garden. 'If God allows the Robber family to see this miracle there must be some good in them. Will you not give the Robber Father a free pardon and a chance to live and work like our people? As it is, their children are growing up rough and wild. If we are not careful we shall have a young Robber gang up there in the Great Forest, and then there will be trouble.'

'There is some truth in what you say, good father Abbot,' said the Bishop. 'Not that I believe this story of the Christmas garden. However, you can go and look for it if you wish, and if you bring me back one of those silver and gold flowers, I'll grant the Robber a free pardon with pleasure.'

Well, Christmas Eve came at last. The good old Abbot asked his gardener to go with him into the Great Forest, and there, under the old oak, waited the eldest Robber Son. The gardener muttered angrily under his breath as they followed the boy through the dark forest. He had not wanted to leave his warm home on Christmas Eve. He thought of his cosy chair beside the fire, and he wished he was sitting in it, watching his wife pluck the turkey and his children decorate the Christmas tree. He did not believe in the Christmas garden and thought the whole expedition was stupid. However, he dared not disobey his old master and he was too fond of him to do so.

On and on they tramped through the snow till they came to a cave. They followed the boy through an opening into a cavern where the Robber Mother was sitting beside a log fire. The Robber children sprawled about the floor playing with small stones, while Robber Father lay stretched out on a pile of dried bracken.

'Sit down by the fire and warm yourself, Lord Abbot,' said Robber Mother. 'You can sleep if you're tired. I'll keep watch and I'll wake you when it is time to see what you have come to see.'

'I'll keep watch too,' said the gardener, who still did not trust the Robber family.

The old Abbot thanked the woman and stretched himself on the ground beside the fire and fell asleep. He was so tired.

He had not slept long when he woke to hear the chimes of the Christmas bells. The gardener helped him to his feet and they followed the Robber family to the entrance of the cave.

'It is extraordinary to be able to hear the Christmas bells here in the forest. I wouldn't have thought it possible,' said the Abbot.

'Ah well, everything looks the same as ever out here,' grumbled the gardener, who was still in a bad temper.

It was true, the forest was as dark and gloomy as before, but instead of an icy wind, they felt a warm gentle breeze and a strange stirring all about them. Suddenly the bells stopped ringing. And then it happened.

The darkness turned into a pink dawn. The snow melted from the ground, leaving emerald shoots that grew before their eyes. Ferns sent up their fronds, curled like a bishop's staff, and spring flowers carpeted the earth. Trees burst into leaf and then into blossom. Butterflies and birds darted from tree to tree, and there was a soft hum of insects.

The Robber children laughed and rolled in the grass while Robber Mother and Robber Father stared wide-eyed and smiling. They too seemed transformed. And there, at his feet, the Abbot saw the silver and gold flower of the Christmas rose. He was filled with happiness and he knelt down and thanked God for allowing him to see such a miracle.

This seemed to make the gardener more angry than ever.

'This is no miracle,' he said in a loud voice, 'this is witchcraft and the work of the devil!'

As he said this darkness fell and an icy wind blew snow through the forest. The Robber family ran shivering into the cave, but the old Abbot stumbled forward on his face, clutching at the earth as he fell. The garden vanished, leaving the forest as dark and gloomy as ever.

The gardener hoisted the Abbot on to his back and carried him back to the monastery. There he was laid on his bed. The monks all marvelled at the radiant smile on his still face. At least he had died with a happy heart, they told each other.

Now, the old Abbot was found to have the root of a plant clutched in one hand. It was given to the gardener who planted it carefully in the Abbot's garden. Every day he went to see if it was growing, but although there were green leaves there were no signs of a flower in the spring, nor in the summer, and autumn passed and there was not even a bud to be seen. The gardener wondered if it would ever flower.

Then on Christmas morning, when the ground was sprinkled with snow, the gardener saw a beautiful cluster of silvery white flowers growing from the plant, their frail petals surrounding the pale golden stamens. He had seen the flower only once before, in that Christmas garden of the Great Forest. It must be the Christmas rose, and the good Abbot had managed to pluck one after all.

At once the gardener knew what he must do. He picked three of the white flowers and took them to the Bishop.

'My Lord Bishop,' said the gardener, 'our father Abbot sends you these flowers as he promised.'

Then he told the Bishop about the wonderful Christmas garden and all that had happened in the Great Forest that Christmas Eve.

'The good Abbot kept his promise and I shall keep mine,' said the Bishop, and he wrote a free pardon for the Robber Father there and then.

The gardener took the pardon to the Robber Father but when he reached the cave he found the entrance barred against him.

'Go away!' roared Robber Father. 'Thanks to you there was no wonderful garden here this Christmas Eve. Go away, unless you want a fight!'

'You're right, it was my fault; I had no faith. I was wrong but you must allow me to deliver your free pardon from the Bishop. You are free, and from now on you may return to the village and live and work among the people.'

And so it was that the Robber family left the Great Forest and were able to enjoy Christmas in their own home, with all their friends around them.

Not Just for Christmas

ROB CHILDS

JAMES WOKE up very early with an extra special sense of excitement.

Christmas Day! He felt like shouting it out. He had been looking forward to this day for so long, and now – at last – it was here!

Trembling, James sat up in bed and rubbed his eyes. He opened them again, slowly, but everywhere was dark and he still couldn't see anything.

He tried not to be too disappointed. 'Maybe they're with all my other presents,' he murmured. 'Santa must have been by now.'

James liked to talk to himself, to hear the sound of his voice in the darkness. He was glad he had his own bedroom. It was his private little world, a place where he knew that nobody else would be nearby to listen. Like Hannah, for instance.

His sister was OK to play with at times, he admitted, but she was only five, three years younger than him. Her never-ending chatter often irritated him, especially if she got too big for her boots and tried to do things for him.

'I wonder where everything will be this year?' he said aloud.

It was part of the family fun at Christmas. After Santa's visit, Mum and Dad would hide the presents all over the house and then go back to sleep. He and Hannah had to wait, bursting with anticipation, until their parents said they could start looking. James considered whether he might risk going to wake them up yet so he could begin the hunt.

'Bet it's still a bit too early.'

He reached under the pillows instead for his favourite toy soldier, but his fingers first touched a piece of paper. It was a copy of his letter to Santa, put there for safe keeping, and he gave it a superstitious pat.

Then his hand closed around the small plastic figure with a gun and he whipped it out with a flourish. 'Bang!' he cried, pretending to shoot at the one-eared teddy bear that lay by his side. 'Bang! Bang!'

He chuckled as Teddy had to dive down on to the carpet to escape the bullets. James leaped out of bed after him and the fight went on as Sam the soldier chased Teddy across the floor.

'Oooh! It's too cold!' James said, with a shiver. He grabbed Teddy and scrambled back under the duvet, wriggling right down until he was completely covered. Snuggling up with Teddy, he felt warm again and happy, hoping it wouldn't be long before he'd be able to see all the pretty lights on the Christmas tree. He closed his eyes and crossed his fingers.

'James! James! Wake up!'

He was being pushed and pulled about, but he stayed underneath the thick duvet out of sight.

'I *am* awake,' came his muffled voice. 'Go away!'

'You were fast asleep,' Hannah insisted. 'I was awake before you.'

His tousled head shot out from the covers. 'No, you weren't. I've been awake for years.'

'No, you haven't! I was up first this morning.'

'Rubbish! I even helped Santa empty his sack!'

Hannah gave up. She could never win such silly arguments with her stubborn big brother.

'It's time!' she announced instead.

James knew exactly what she meant. 'I know,' he replied. 'I was just waiting for you, that's all, so we went in together.'

She gave him a funny look, but knew that all the faces she might pull were just wasted on James. 'Come on then. Let's go in!'

Tingling with excitement, the children crept along the landing and pushed open the door to their parents' bedroom.

'Dad's snoring,' James hissed.

'Goodie!' giggled Hannah. 'We can both sneak up on him and make him jump!'

James felt his sister's hand slide into his as they tiptoed into the room towards Dad's side of the bed.

'Oh no, you don't, you two!' came a voice in the darkness. 'I know what you're up to!'

'Mummy!' Hannah squealed. 'Oh, you spoiled it!'

Mum laughed. 'You little pests. Do you know what time it is?'

'No,' said James, 'but I do know what day it is. It's Christmas Day!'

'Come on in,' Mum invited them, drawing back the duvet covers. 'Come and have a Christmas cuddle.'

Hannah slithered in front for a kiss from Mum, quickly followed by James. Dad rolled over. 'Who's the elephant with cold feet?' he grumbled sleepily.

'James, Daddy!' Hannah cried. 'Happy Christmas!'

'Christmas is cancelled!'

'No, it's not!' they chorused.

'Yes, it is,' he said. 'Haven't you heard? Santa's gone on holiday!'

'No, he hasn't. You're just teasing,' James chuckled, punching Dad on the shoulder. 'He only goes on holiday after he's delivered all our presents. It's time now.'

'It's time, Mummy,' echoed Hannah. 'It's time!'

'I can see we're not going to get any peace,' Mum said. 'OK, it's time. Off you go while I make a drink.'

The children whooped their delight and shot out of the bed, desperate to be the one to find the first present. They always knew whose it was by the wrapping. Hannah's gifts had ribbon around them and a bow, while James's were tied up loosely with string. He loved pulling off the string and tearing open the packaging to see what was inside.

'Found one straight away!' he screamed proudly as he squirmed underneath the bed. 'And it's mine!'

He ripped the string and wrapping paper away from the box and held it up to his nose. 'Hmm, yummy smell! My favourite chocs!'

His next discovery, at the bottom of a wardrobe, didn't have anything round it at all. It didn't need it. James knew what it was as soon as he felt around the shoes and touched it. 'Wow! A football. Thanks!'

Dad laughed. 'Santa would have had a terrible job trying to wrap up a football! He obviously didn't bother.'

James stopped searching for anything else for a while, dribbling the ball around the bedroom with his bare feet and knocking into things as he lost control.

'Hey! Steady on, superstar,' cried Dad, getting out of bed himself at last. 'You'll go and break something and then we'll all be in trouble. Let's wait till we get outside in the garden later.'

Shrieks and squeals from Hannah confirmed her own successes, and the children spent a very happy hour up and down the stairs, poking and probing into cupboards and drawers. James even found a tape of one of his best-loved stories lying in the bath.

'Good job I didn't turn the taps on first,' he grinned.

Mum laughed. 'No danger of you volunteering to have a bath, is there, you mucky pup.'

She caught Dad's eye and they smiled at what she had just said. Mum put down her cup of tea and pulled the two children gently towards her on the sofa.

'Uncle John is coming round later this morning,' she said, giving them both a hug. 'He's bringing along something else for you, although it's not really a Christmas present. It's something even more special.'

Hannah's eyes widened. 'Is it a pony?' she gasped.

Mum shook her head and smiled. 'No guessing allowed. We want it to be a surprise.'

Mum supervised their washing and dressing while Dad prepared some breakfast. 'What time is Uncle John coming?' asked Hannah the moment she trotted into the kitchen.

'Soon,' Dad said. 'You'll have to be patient and play with all your new toys until he gets here.'

'Will we be able to play with what he's bringing?' she persisted.

'Still trying to work out what it can be, aren't you?' he laughed. 'But yes, you'll certainly be able to play with it.'

James was strangely quiet at the table, nibbling at a piece of toast, and Dad attempted to cheer him up. 'How about us two going out to kick your new ball about a bit, eh?'

James nodded, but didn't look up. 'Have I found *all* my presents yet?' he asked instead.

'Not quite,' Mum replied. 'I think there are still a couple of things hidden away.'

'I'll help him look for them,' Hannah piped up.

'No you won't!' cried James. 'I don't need any help. I'll find them when I'm ready.'

Hannah was about to answer him back until Mum shot her a warning glance and she swiftly changed the subject. 'This is the best Christmas ever,' she beamed. 'I've got everything I wanted. Have you, James?'

'Not yet,' he said simply and slid away from the table to play with the toy cars that he'd left near the fire.

When the bell rang, the children rushed to the door, both wanting to be the one to open it. Hannah won the race – as usual.

'Hi, kids!' Uncle John greeted them. 'Merry Christmas, everyone!'

Hannah looked all around for whatever it was that Uncle John was supposed to have with him. There was nothing to be seen.

'Did you like my presents I got Santa to leave for you?' he asked and then laughed at their blank expressions. 'Just like me when I was your age. Too busy opening the boxes to bother with the labels!'

'Uncle John bought you those horrible noisy, electronic games,' Dad explained, slipping his younger brother a wink. 'Typical! He won't be the one who's got to put up with all the din every time you play with them.'

'Oh, thank you, Uncle John!' Hannah said politely as he picked her up to give her a peck on the cheek.

'Thanks, I'll have some fun with that, annoying Dad,' grinned James.

Uncle John acted as though he'd just remembered something. 'Oh, yes, I almost forgot. There's another thing you'll have a lot of fun with, too. I've left it in the car.'

Still carrying Hannah, he led the way out on to the drive, and his niece suddenly let out a shriek.

From her high vantage point, she could see into the back of his estate car. 'A puppy! A real puppy!'

She squirmed out of his grasp and ran to the car to stare through the rear window. 'Oh, it's beautiful. It's so cute. What big eyes!'

'It's a *she*,' Uncle John said. 'And she's not so cute when she leaves little puddles all over your carpet and inside your car!'

The children laughed and demanded the car be open so that they could hold the puppy.

'Thanks for looking after her for a couple of days, John,' Mum said. 'Hope she hasn't been too much trouble to you.'

'None at all,' he grinned. 'Apart from the puddles!'

'What is she?' asked James.

'A labrador,' said Dad. 'And she's just seven weeks old.'

James stroked the puppy's short, stubby nose and chin as Hannah cuddled her. 'What shall we call her?' he wondered.

'Actually, she's already got a name,' said Mum. 'It's Misty.'

'Who gave her that?'

'The people at the kennels where she was born.'

James considered it for a moment. 'OK, Misty's a fine name.'

Mum smiled with relief. 'Do you like her?' she asked anxiously.

He nodded. 'I've often wanted a dog to play with.'

'I know, but we weren't quite sure if it would be a good thing,' Dad said. 'Especially after that big dog down the street knocked you over.'

'It wasn't the dog's fault,' James said. 'I must have stepped on its tail or something and hurt it.'

'You cried,' gloated his sister. 'I remember you crying.'

'So?' he demanded. 'You would have done too. You're always crying. It just made me jump, that's all. I didn't know what was happening.'

'Anyway, never mind now, don't argue,' Mum said, prising the puppy out of Hannah's arms. 'Let James hold Misty for a while, darling.'

Hannah looked down at her dress in dismay. 'Oh! I'm all wet!'

Everyone laughed. 'Serves you right for squeezing her so tight,' Dad chuckled.

'Let's take Misty into the back garden and play ball,' said James as Mum led Hannah into the house to change her clothes.

His new football was far too big for the puppy and James kicked a small ball across the lawn instead. It was ideal. The ball made a rattling sound as it rolled along, attracting her attention, and Misty scampered after it with yelps of excitement.

Dad and Uncle John joined in the game, laughing at the puppy's antics. The ball was just the right size for Misty and light enough for her to nose it through the grass in a wayward dribble. Dad passed the rattling ball to James who timed his next kick perfectly, sending it flying into the bushes by the fence.

'Goal!' cried Uncle John. 'Great stuff, James. We'll have you playing for United yet.'

'Rovers!' James corrected him. 'They're the best team in the land.'

The puppy soon grew weary. She squatted on the lawn and then settled down for a nap.

'Dog-tired! Just like the Rovers' players,' joked Uncle John to tease James again about his favourite football team.

Dad carried Misty inside for a drink of water from the shiny metal bowl that his brother had also brought with him. She lapped noisily at the water, spilling most of it on to the kitchen floor.

'Looks like we'll get through a lot of newspapers, soaking up all her messes,' Mum chuckled. 'I just hope Misty realizes what a lucky puppy she is, coming to live with us until she grows up.'

'Till she grows up?' repeated James in alarm. 'What do you mean?'

Mum put her arm around his shoulders and led him through to the lounge, calling Hannah to join them. As the family sat together near the Christmas tree, Misty curled up asleep on the rug in front of the fire.

'Misty doesn't know it yet,' Mum said, 'but when she's older and specially trained, she's going to have a very important job to do.'

'What's that?' James interrupted impatiently, but the answer stunned him into silence.

'She will become a guide dog for a blind person.'

Dad picked up the story. 'But while she's a puppy, she needs to be looked after and loved just like any normal pet. That's where we come in. We've decided to be puppy-walkers.'

'Puppy-walkers!' giggled Hannah. 'What a funny name!'

'Perhaps it is,' Mum smiled, 'because we'll be doing far more than just walking Misty. She'll be one of the family for a whole year.'

'But then has she got to go to somebody else?' asked James.

'I'm afraid so,' Dad answered. 'But we can always take on another puppy after that, if we want to.'

'We thought it might be better this way at first,' Mum explained. 'Just to let you get used to having a dog around the house. See how you get on together.'

'We'll get on just fine,' he said seriously. 'I've never heard of people being puppy-walkers. It's a good idea.'

James lay down next to the puppy on the rug, stroking her soft fur and gently fondling her large, floppy ears. He was rewarded with little grunts of contentment, almost like purring, and then felt his hand being licked by a rasping, wet tongue.

'Ooh! It tickles!' he chuckled.

Hannah didn't intend to be left out. She wanted to be licked too, and Misty rolled her tongue along the girl's bare arm as far as she could reach, sending Hannah into fits of giggles.

'Misty certainly won't be going short of love and fuss here, I can see that,' Uncle John laughed. 'She's fallen on her feet all right – and she knows it!'

As the puppy dozed, Hannah disappeared to try on her new ballet costume, but James stayed at Misty's side, his hand resting on one of her stretched-out legs. 'She feels so warm,' he murmured happily.

'You look wonderful together, lying there,' Mum told him. 'We'll have to take a photo of you both like that.'

There was no chance now. Misty was awake again – and looking for a spot of mischief. She found a willing partner in James, equally eager to play and tumble about.

'Here you are,' said Dad. 'Have one of my old socks to play tug of war with. Dogs love that game.'

'Hope it's a clean one and not too smelly,' laughed James, who soon felt a determined tugging at the other end of the sock.

'Misty doesn't seem to mind anyway,' Dad grinned.

James let Misty win some of the battles, but she always brought the sock straight back, nudging him to grab hold of it again. Then he decided to throw it away for her to fetch.

The sock landed right on top of the Christmas cake on the table.

'Good job your mum didn't see that!' cried Uncle John, lifting it off quickly and returning it to James. 'Try again.'

He did, and this time it went into the trifle!

'I think you're better at kicking than throwing,' said Uncle John.

The sock came back with a little trace of cream which Misty soon found. She licked her lips with pleasure at the taste.

James played with Misty almost all day in between her frequent snoozes and feeding times. He even forgot to search for his remaining presents until just before bedtime. He wanted Misty to sleep in his bedroom with him as well, but Mum had to be very firm about that.

'She's better off in the kitchen,' Mum said. 'She needs a place of her own at night too, just like you. And I can put plenty of newspaper all over the floor there around her dog basket!'

Mum sat on the side of his bed and read him a story. 'Have you enjoyed having a puppy to play with?' she asked, before saying goodnight.

James nodded several times. 'We're going to have great fun, Misty and me, while she's with us. I can teach her lots of things.'

'Yes, like how to get into all sorts of trouble, no doubt,' Mum laughed. 'And how to get all mucky!'

'Can I have a dog of my own one day?'

'Of course. When you're older. You'll be able to go everywhere together then.'

James grinned. 'I'll call mine Sam.'

'Why Sam?'

James shrugged, unwilling to admit to his soldier's name. 'I just like the sound of it.'

Mum bent over to kiss him and caught sight of a piece of paper sticking out from underneath his pillow. She guessed what it was. James had insisted on having a copy of the letter she'd written to Santa for him. Mum remembered off by heart the words that he'd wanted her to write, but she couldn't resist the temptation to read them again now.

Mum quietly slid the paper away from the pillow without James realizing what she was doing. He lay with a happy, peaceful expression on his face, his eyes closed.

A few silent tears escaped from hers as she read over the short letter:

Dear Santa,

I hope you are well. My name is James and I am eight years old. Please can I have a new pair of eyes at Christmas? I keep bumping into things. I know this will be difficult, but I'm sure you will find a way of doing it somehow.

Thank you very much.
Love James

P.S. It would even be nice to see my pesky little sister as well.

Mum slipped the paper back into place and kissed James again. That lovely picture of him lying cosily beside Misty in the glow of the fire swam into her mind. 'I'm so glad you like your new pair of eyes, my darling,' she whispered.

He smiled and his eyes flickered open, staring up at her blindly.

Author's note:

The Guide Dogs for the Blind Association run puppy-walking schemes in many parts of the country. Families take a puppy, usually a labrador or a golden retriever, into their home to rear as an ordinary pet for the first year of its life. The young dog then goes to a special training centre to learn how to become a guide dog. There is no longer a lower age limit for owning a guide dog (www.guidedogs.org.uk/services-we-provide).

Marley's Ghost

from *A Christmas Carol*, first published in 1843

CHARLES DICKENS

SCROOGE TOOK his melancholy dinner in his usual melancholy tavern; and having read all the newspapers, and beguiled the rest of the evening with his banker's-book, went home to bed. He lived in chambers which had once belonged to his deceased partner. They were a gloomy suite of rooms, in a lowering pile of building up a yard ... It was old enough now, and dreary enough, for nobody lived in it but Scrooge, the other rooms being all let out as offices. The yard was so dark that even Scrooge, who knew its every stone, was fain to grope with his hands. The fog and frost so hung about the black old gateway of the house that it seemed as if the Genius of the Weather sat in mournful meditation on the threshold.

Now, it is a fact that there was nothing at all particular about the knocker on the door, except that it was very large. It is also a fact that Scrooge had seen it night and morning during his whole residence in that place; also that Scrooge had as little of what is called fancy about him as any man in the City of London, even including – which is a bold word – the corporation, aldermen, and livery. Let it also be borne in mind that Scrooge had not bestowed one thought on Marley, since his last mention of his seven-years' dead partner that afternoon. And then let any man explain to me, if he can, how it happened that Scrooge, having his key in the lock of the door, saw in the knocker, without its undergoing any intermediate process of change, not a knocker, but Marley's face.

Marley's face. It was not in impenetrable shadow, as the other objects in the yard were, but had a dismal light about it, like a bad lobster in a dark cellar. It was not angry or ferocious, but looked at Scrooge as Marley used to look: with ghostly spectacles turned up upon its ghostly forehead. The hair was curiously stirred, as if by breath or hot air; and though the eyes were wide open, they were perfectly motionless. That, and its livid colour, made it horrible; but its horror seemed to be in spite of the face and beyond its control, rather than a part of its own expression.

As Scrooge looked fixedly at this phenomenon, it was a knocker again.

To say that he was not startled, or that his blood was not conscious of a terrible sensation to which it had been a stranger from infancy, would be untrue. But he put his hand upon the key he had relinquished, turned it sturdily, walked in, and lighted his candle.

He *did* pause, with a moment's irresolution, before he shut the door; and he *did* look cautiously behind it first, as if he half-expected to be terrified with the sight of Marley's pigtail sticking out into the hall. But there was nothing on the back of the door, except the screws and nuts that held the knocker on, so he said, 'Pooh, pooh!' and closed it with a bang.

The sound resounded through the house like thunder. Every room above, and every cask in the wine-merchant's cellars below, appeared to have a separate peal of echoes of its own. Scrooge was not a man to be frightened by echoes. He fastened the door, and walked across the hall, and up the stairs, slowly too, trimming his candle as he went.

You may talk vaguely about driving a coach-and-six up a good old flight of stairs, or through a bad young Act of Parliament; but I mean to say you might have got a hearse up that staircase, and taken it broadwise, with the splinter-bar towards the wall and the door towards the balustrades – and done it easy. There was plenty of width for that, and room to spare; which is perhaps the reason why Scrooge thought he saw a locomotive hearse going on before him in the gloom. Half a dozen gas-lamps out of the streets wouldn't have lighted the entry too well, so you may suppose that it was pretty dark with Scrooge's dip.

Up Scrooge went, not caring a button for that: darkness is cheap, and Scrooge liked it. But before he shut his heavy door, he walked through his rooms to see that all was right. He had just enough recollection of the face to desire to do that.

Sitting-room, bed-room, lumber-room. All as they should be. Nobody under the table, nobody under the sofa; a small fire in the grate; spoon and basin ready; and the little saucepan of gruel (Scrooge had a cold in his head) upon the hob. Nobody under the bed; nobody in the closet; nobody in his dressing-gown, which was hanging up in a suspicious attitude against the wall. Lumber-room as usual. Old fire-guard, old shoes, two fish-baskets, washing-stand on three legs, and a poker.

Quite satisfied, he closed his door, and locked himself in; double-locked himself in, which was not his custom. Thus secured against surprise, he took off his cravat; put on his dressing-gown and slippers, and his night-cap; and sat down before the fire to take his gruel.

It was a very low fire indeed; nothing on such a bitter night. He was obliged to sit close to it, and brood over it, before he could extract the least sensation of warmth from such a handful of fuel. The fire-place was an old one, built by some Dutch merchant long ago, and paved all round with quaint Dutch tiles, designed to illustrate the Scriptures . . . hundreds of figures, to attract his thoughts; and yet that face of Marley, seven years dead, came like the ancient Prophet's rod, and swallowed up the whole. If each smooth tile had been a blank at first, with power to shape some picture on its surface from the disjointed fragments of his thoughts, there would have been a copy of old Marley's head on every one.

'Humbug!' said Scrooge, and walked across the room.

After several turns, he sat down again. As he threw his head back in the chair, his glance happened to rest upon a bell, a disused bell, that hung in the room, and communicated for some purpose now forgotten with a chamber in the highest storey of the building. It was with great astonishment, and with a strange, inexplicable dread, that as he looked, he saw this bell begin to swing. It swung so softly in the outset that it scarcely made a sound; but soon it rang out loudly, and so did every bell in the house.

This might have lasted half a minute, or a minute, but it seemed an hour. The bells ceased as they had begun, together. They were succeeded by a clanking noise, deep down below; as if some person were dragging a heavy chain over the casks in the wine-merchant's cellar. Scrooge then remembered to have heard that ghosts in haunted houses were described as dragging chains.

The cellar-door flew open with a booming sound, and then he heard the noise much louder, on the floors below; then coming up the stairs; then coming straight towards his door.

'It's humbug still!' said Scrooge. 'I won't believe it.'

His colour changed though, when, without a pause, it came on through the heavy door, and passed into the room before his eyes. Upon its coming in, the dying flame leaped up, as though it cried, 'I know him! Marley's Ghost!' and fell again.

The same face: the very same. Marley in his pigtail, usual waistcoat, tights, and boots; the tassels on the latter bristling, like his pigtail, and his coat-skirts, and the hair upon his head. The chain he drew was clasped about his middle. It was long, and wound about him like a tail; and it was made (for Scrooge observed it closely) of cash-boxes, keys, padlocks, ledgers, deeds, and heavy purses wrought in steel. His body was transparent, so that Scrooge, observing him, and looking through his waistcoat, could see the two buttons on his coat behind.

Scrooge had often heard it said that Marley had no bowels, but he had never believed it until now.

No, nor did he believe it even now. Though he looked the phantom through and through, and saw it standing before him; though he felt the chilling influence of its death-cold eyes; and marked the very texture of the folded kerchief bound about its head and chin, which wrapper he had not observed before; he was still incredulous, and fought against his senses.

'How now!' said Scrooge, caustic and cold as ever. 'What do you want with me?'

'Much!' – Marley's voice, no doubt about it.

'Who are you?'

'Ask me who I *was*.'

'Who *were* you then?' said Scrooge, raising his voice. 'You're particular – for a shade.' He was going to say '*to* a shade,' but substituted this, as more appropriate.

'In life I was your partner, Jacob Marley.'

'Can you – can you sit down?' asked Scrooge, looking doubtfully at him.

'I can.'

'Do it then.'

Scrooge asked the question, because he didn't know whether a ghost so transparent might find himself in a condition to take a chair; and felt that in the event of its being impossible, it might involve the necessity of an embarrassing explanation. But the ghost sat down on the opposite side of the fire-place, as if he were quite used to it.

'You don't believe in me,' observed the Ghost.

'I don't,' said Scrooge.

'What evidence would you have of my reality beyond that of your senses?'

'I don't know,' said Scrooge.

'Why do you doubt your senses?'

'Because,' said Scrooge, 'a little thing affects them. A slight disorder of the stomach makes them cheats. You may be an undigested bit of beef, a blot of mustard, a crumb of cheese, a fragment of an underdone potato. There's more of gravy than of grave about you, whatever you are!'

Scrooge was not much in the habit of cracking jokes, nor did he feel, in his heart, by any means waggish then. The truth is that he tried to be smart, as a means of distracting his own attention, and keeping down his terror; for the spectre's voice disturbed the very marrow in his bones . . .

'You see this toothpick?' said Scrooge . . .

'I do,' replied the Ghost.

'You are not looking at it,' said Scrooge.

'But I see it,' said the Ghost, 'notwithstanding.'

'Well!' returned Scrooge. 'I have but to swallow this, and be for the rest of my days persecuted by a legion of goblins, all of my own creation. Humbug, I tell you; humbug!'

At this, the spirit raised a frightful cry, and shook its chain with such a dismal and appalling noise that Scrooge held on tight to his chair, to save himself from falling in a swoon. But how much greater was his horror when the phantom, taking off the bandage round its head, as if it were too warm to wear in-doors, its lower jaw dropped down upon its breast!

Scrooge fell upon his knees, and clasped his hands before his face.

'Mercy!' he said. 'Dreadful apparition, why do you trouble me?'

'Man of the worldly mind,' replied the Ghost, 'do you believe in me or not?'

'I do,' said Scrooge. 'I must. But why do spirits walk the earth, and why do they come to me?'

'It is required of every man,' the Ghost returned, 'that the spirit within him should walk abroad among his fellowmen, and travel far and wide; and if that spirit goes not forth in life, it is condemned to do so after death. It is doomed to wander through the world – oh, woe is me! – and witness that it cannot share, but might have shared on earth, and turned to happiness!'

Again the spectre raised a cry, and shook its chain, and wrung its shadowy hands.

'You are fettered,' said Scrooge, trembling. 'Tell me why?'

'I wear the chain I forged in life,' replied the Ghost. 'I made it link by link, and yard by yard; I girded it on of my own free will, and of my own free will I wore it. Is its pattern strange to *you*?'

Scrooge trembled more and more.

'Or would you know,' pursued the Ghost, 'the weight and length of the strong coil you bear yourself? It was full as heavy and as long as this, seven Christmas Eves ago. You have laboured on it, since. It is a ponderous chain!'

Scrooge glanced about him on the floor, in the expectation of finding himself surrounded by some fifty or sixty fathoms of iron cable; but he could see nothing.

'Jacob,' he said, imploringly. 'Old Jacob Marley, tell me more. Speak comfort to me, Jacob.'

'I have none to give,' the Ghost replied. 'It comes from other regions, Ebenezer Scrooge, and is conveyed by other ministers, to other kinds of men. Nor can I tell you what I would. A very little more is all permitted to me. I cannot rest, I cannot stay, I cannot linger anywhere. My spirit never walked beyond our counting-house – mark me! – in life my spirit never roved beyond the narrow limits of our money-changing hole; and weary journeys lie before me!'

It was a habit with Scrooge, whenever he became thoughtful, to put his hands in his breeches pockets. Pondering on what the Ghost had said, he did so now, but without lifting up his eyes, or getting off his knees . . .

'But you were always a good man of business, Jacob,' faltered Scrooge, who now began to apply this to himself.

'Business!' cried the Ghost, wringing his hands again. 'Mankind was my business. The common welfare was my business; charity, mercy, forbearance and benevolence were, all, my business. The dealings of my trade were but a drop of water in the comprehensive ocean of my business!'

It held up its chain at arm's length, as if that were the cause of all its unavailing grief, and flung it heavily upon the ground again.

'At this time of the rolling year,' the spectre said, 'I suffer most. Why did I walk through crowds of fellow-beings with my eyes turned down, and never raise them to that blessed Star which led the Wise Men to a poor abode? Were there no poor homes to which its light would have conducted *me*!'

Scrooge was very much dismayed to hear the spectre going on at this rate, and began to quake exceedingly.

'Hear me!' cried the Ghost. 'My time is nearly gone.'

'I will,' said Scrooge. 'But don't be hard upon me! Don't be flowery, Jacob! Pray!'

'How it is that I appear before you in a shape that you can see, I may not tell. I have sat invisible beside you many and many a day.'

It was not an agreeable idea. Scrooge shivered, and wiped the perspiration from his brow.

'There is no light part of my penance,' pursued the Ghost. 'I am here tonight to warn you that you have yet a chance and hope of escaping my fate. A chance and hope of my procuring, Ebenezer.'

'You were always a good friend to me,' said Scrooge. 'Thank'ee!'

'You will be haunted,' resumed the Ghost, 'by Three Spirits.'

Scrooge's countenance fell almost as low as the Ghost's had done.

'Is that the chance and hope you mentioned, Jacob?' he demanded, in a faltering voice.

'It is.'

'I – I think I'd rather not,' said Scrooge.

'Without their visits,' said the Ghost, 'you cannot hope to shun the path I tread. Expect the first tomorrow, when the bell tolls One.'

'Couldn't I take 'em all at once, and have it over, Jacob?' hinted Scrooge.

'Expect the second on the next night at the same hour. The third upon the next night when the last stroke of Twelve has ceased to vibrate. Look to see no more; and look that, for your own sake, you remember what has passed between us!'

When it had said these words, the spectre took its wrapper from the table and bound it round its head, as before. Scrooge knew this, by the smart sound its teeth made, when the jaws were brought together by the bandage. He ventured to raise his eyes again, and found his supernatural visitor confronting him in an erect attitude, with its chain wound over and about its arm.

The apparition walked backward from him; and at every step it took, the window raised itself a little, so that when the spectre reached it, it was wide open. It beckoned Scrooge to approach, which he did. When they were within two paces of each other, Marley's Ghost held up its hand, warning him to come no nearer. Scrooge stopped.

Not so much in obedience, as in surprise and fear: for on the raising of the hand, he became sensible of confused noises in the air; incoherent sounds of lamentation and regret; wailings inexpressibly sorrowful and self-accusatory. The spectre, after listening for a moment, joined in the mournful dirge; and floated out upon the bleak, dark night.

Scrooge followed to the window, desperate in his curiosity. He looked out.

The air was filled with phantoms, wandering hither and thither in restless haste, and moaning as they went. Every one of them wore chains like Marley's Ghost; some few (they might be guilty governments) were linked together; none were free. Many had been personally known to Scrooge in their lives. He had been quite familiar with one old ghost in a white waistcoat, with a monstrous iron safe attached to its ankle, who cried piteously at being unable to assist a wretched woman with an infant, whom it saw below, upon a doorstep. The misery with them all was, clearly, that they sought to interfere, for good, in human matters, and had lost the power for ever.

Whether these creatures faded into mist, or mist enshrouded them, he could not tell. But they and their spirit voices faded together; and the night became as it had been when he walked home.

Scrooge closed the window, and examined the door by which the Ghost had entered. It was double-locked, as he had locked it with his own hands, and the bolts were undisturbed. He tried to say 'Humbug!' but stopped at the first syllable. And being, from the emotion he had undergone, or the fatigues of the day, or his glimpse of the Invisible World, or the dull conversation of the Ghost, or the lateness of the hour, much in need of repose, went straight to bed, without undressing, and fell asleep upon the instant.

Simon and the Snow

GINO ALBERTI

SIMON LIVED in a little house high up in the mountains. It was winter and he was happy, for of all the seasons he loved winter the best.

He loved the snowflakes and the icicles; he loved to take long rides on his sledge, and most of all he loved to build jolly round snowmen with carrot noses.

One day Simon looked around him and noticed grass growing and new buds on the trees. Spring had come early.

Simon was sad: he wished it could be winter for ever.

But that night, as Simon lay sleeping, the air turned cold again. Softly, it began to snow.

The garden was covered in white and the windows were speckled with frost.

As soon as Simon woke up, he noticed that something was different.

He ran to the window and looked out in wonder at the snow. The winter had come back again! It was as if his wish had come true.

'The snow is back! The snow is back!' he cried out joyfully. He put on his woolly hat and mittens and ran outside. He began to build a whole family of snowmen. His mother gave him some carrots for the noses and some straw for the arms. Simon was very happy.

The next day was even colder. As soon as he was up, Simon went to play with his snow family. But what had happened? He ran from one snowman to the next. The twig arms and the carrot noses were gone! Who could have done such a thing?

There was no time to think for Simon's mother was calling him in to breakfast. Later, as Simon fetched some new noses and arms from the kitchen, he made a plan.

That night the sky was so clear you could count the stars. While his mother slept, Simon wrapped up warmly, collected his cat Mutz and climbed out through the window. Together they trudged through the snow until they came to a very tall tree. 'Here's a good place,' said Simon as he climbed up. Mutz followed. They were cold and frightened, but even if they had to stay up all night they would catch the carrot thieves.

For a long, long while everything was still. Then, suddenly, Simon saw something move. Gathering up his courage he climbed down the tree and hid behind a snowman. He could hardly believe his eyes – all kinds of animals were coming out of the forest and they were greedily eating everything they could from the snowmen.

Simon could see that the poor animals were very thin and hungry. The return of the winter had buried their food under deep snow. He quietly took a couple of steps towards them, but the animals ran away in fright.

Later that morning, Simon told his mother what had happened. 'The poor animals are starving,' she said, and she gave him a basket of hay to take to them.

Simon carried the basket to the edge of the forest. The animals gazed at him hungrily. 'Don't be frightened,' Simon whispered.

Very, very slowly a little deer dared to come forward. Then, when the other animals saw it was safe, they too came out of the forest. There were fawns and rabbits and stags and birds. Simon fed as many as he could, but there wasn't enough food for everyone. Then Simon had an idea.

He put the basket on his back and set off to the village. Shyly, the animals followed him. The village people stopped what they were doing to watch the strange little procession making its way down the mountain.

Everyone wanted to hear Simon's story. He told them about his snowmen and how he had discovered the hungry animals. The whole village wanted to help. At the entrance to the village the grown-ups built a big feeding trough. Then all the children ran home to fetch food for the animals.

Every day, the children brought new supplies. There was enough for all.

Soon the snow melted and the days began to grow warmer. The smell of new grass was in the air again. Spring had come at last – this time to stay. The animals could go back to the forest for good.

From that time on, Simon still loved the winter, but now he loved the spring as well, for he knew the importance of the seasons.

Baboushka

inspired by a Russian folktale

RETOLD BY CAITLIN MATTHEWS

MANY YEARS ago, in the land of Russia, there lived a woman called Baboushka. Her house was the most beautifully kept in the whole village. From the brightly coloured gables on her wooden roof, right down to her neat little garden, her house was a sight to behold.

Although she lived alone, Baboushka was forever washing and cleaning, baking and cooking, painting and gardening, as if she was expecting a special guest. Although she was past the age of motherhood, she especially loved children and she spent the long, cold winter months making fine little toys. Her hands were clever and strong, and her heart was pure and generous. Everyone in the village was very fond of her.

One evening, in the great expanse of the heavens, there appeared an enormous star with a trailing tail that moved across the sky. Everyone in the village was very excited about the new star, wondering what it could mean, but Baboushka merely smiled and shook her head. 'Whatever it means, there is still the floor to be washed and the bread to be baked.'

But the very next day, the meaning became plain. Over the hills beyond the village came a procession of strangers. They had come from very far off. In the procession were three mighty kings. There was bearded Caspar in his crown of gold, riding upon a high-stepping black horse. There was Melchior in his robes of white, fastened by a jewel shaped like a star, riding upon a fine camel. And there was Balthasar in his gold and red tunic, seated upon a magnificent white stallion. Each of the kings carried a special treasure.

The kings' servants rode down into the village to find lodgings. They sought out the headman and asked him which house was most fitting for their royal masters to sleep throughout that day, for the kings could travel only by night. The headman longed to invite these grand visitors to his own house, but he knew that it was too small and not fine enough. He had fourteen children and the house was often noisy and not always as clean as it might be. So he said to the servants, 'Tell your royal masters to ask at the house with the coloured gables.'

The kings dismounted outside Baboushka's house and knocked on the door. 'Good woman,' they said as she opened the door, 'we need to rest here this day until the star once more appears in the sky. Do we have your leave to enter?'

Baboushka pressed her hands to her cheeks in astonishment. 'Sirs, please come in. You are most welcome!'

Soon the three kings were sitting at her table and enjoying a meal of freshly cooked bread, beetroot soup, pickled herrings and vegetables, all washed down with birch-sap beer.

When they had eaten, Baboushka invited them to sit around her fire and tell her about their journey.

'We are following the star whose glory has been foretold by my people for many years,' said

Melchior, the firelight playing upon the starry jewel at his breast.

'Where does it lead?' asked Baboushka.

Caspar spoke from the depths of his beard. 'We believe that the star will lead us to a king who is about to be born.'

Balthasar's dark eyes flashed. 'A king who is King of all the Universe. And we have brought him gifts.'

Baboushka's eyes fell upon the precious things that the kings had brought with them, and her heart was strangely moved. If these great kings from countries far away thought it important enough to leave their kingdoms to find a humble newborn baby, then that child must be King indeed. If he were greater than they, then he was her King too.

'I wish I could bring him a present,' she said, almost to herself.

'Then why don't you come with us?' suggested Balthasar.

Baboushka looked up, startled, not realizing that she had uttered her wish aloud.

While they slept soundly, Baboushka cleaned away the meal and tidied up the house. So many guests had left her with much more work than

usual. Could she really leave home and travel with
the three kings? What should she take as a gift?
What things would she need for the journey?

At twilight, she wakened the sleeping kings,
who made ready to leave. Balthasar stretched out
his hand to include her in their procession. 'Are
you coming, Baboushka?'

'I have to find a gift. There is so much to get
ready. I must tidy the house before I go. I will
catch you up.'

The kings went on their way, following the star.

When she looked up and saw the star with her
own eyes, Baboushka knew that she really had
to go. She rushed back into the house and began to
look through her store of gifts. There were wooden
animals, carved and painted; there were birch-
bark boxes filled with ribbons, polished stones and
sweets; there were nesting dolls that sat inside each
other; there were whistles made of reeds. Which
would be good enough for a newborn king?

Baboushka simply could not decide which was
best, so she packed all of them in a big basket. She
could make her decision as she travelled, or else
create something lovely along the way. By the
time she had found her knife and paints, her
scissors and threads, and packed them away with

her own few things for the journey, she heard the sound of the cockerel crowing that dawn was coming. She gave a great big yawn. How tired she was! She had been awake for a day and a night without sleep and now she fell into a deep slumber.

Baboushka woke up at twilight and rushed out with her basket, keeping the glorious star ever before her. In every village, she asked after the three kings and which way they had gone.

Wherever she asked, people would direct her on to the next village or town, pointing the way that the star was travelling. Baboushka trudged onwards for days and months until she came to the royal palace of Jerusalem.

'At last! This must be where the newborn king will be found,' Baboushka thought. She asked a guard outside the walls but he said, 'Yes, the three kings came here but they soon departed, hurrying onwards to a poor little place called Bethlehem.'

Off she went at once. She arrived at twilight and saw how the great star seemed to be directly overhead. Her heart leaped. This must be the place! At the inn she asked the innkeeper, 'Have the three kings been here?'

'Yes. They came to see the baby that was born in the stable here. But the kings have gone home now.'

'And the baby?' asked Baboushka, with a trembling voice.

'Oh, the baby and his family went away as well – to Egypt, I think,' said the innkeeper. Then, seeing her disappointment, he added, 'I can show you the place where the baby was, if you like?'

Baboushka raised tear-filled eyes and followed him to the stable behind the inn. It was like a dimly lit cave inside. 'There is where his mother laid him, in the straw of the manger,' said the innkeeper. 'Who would have thought that the Christ-child, Jesus, would be born in my stable?'

When Baboushka heard the baby's name, she fell on her knees. Peering into the straw, she raised some of it to her face and kissed it. She barely heard the innkeeper telling her about the visit of the shepherds who had heard the message of angels, or about the presentation of gifts by the three kings.

At the thought of the gift that she wanted to give the Christ-child, Baboushka rose and thanked the innkeeper. 'I'm going to find him, King Jesus, and give him my gift,' she said.

And, from that day to this, Baboushka journeys on with her basket of toys, asking everywhere she goes for the newborn king. At every house, especially at Christmas, she looks at the children asleep in their beds and leaves a toy, just in case it might be the King of her heart.

Hetty Feather's Christmas

Set in Victorian times

JACQUELINE WILSON

I GOT VERY excited and enthusiastic about Christmas. It had never been an extraordinary occasion at the hospital. We'd each been given a penny and an orange – that was the extent of our Christmas gifts. There had been no lessons, no hours of darning, but there had been a punishingly long session in the chapel that gave us all aching backs and pins and needles in our dangling legs.

I had read about Christmas though, and was convinced that all other folk sat down to huge tables groaning with capons and figgy puddings galore, with a Christmas tree and coloured lanterns and many presents.

I looked around our small, dimly lit cottage, saw our big stewing pot, and sighed at the few coins rattling in my purse. 'How can we make Christmas special, Jem?' I wailed.

'We don't really set so much store by Christmas,' he said. 'Perhaps we can have a bit of stewing beef. That'll make a nice change.'

'It should be a roast,' I wailed. 'And I need to decorate the house to make it pretty. But what are we going to do about presents? I want to give real gifts. Folk will be getting tired of me stitching them silly clothes.'

'Oh, Hetty, you stitch beautiful clothes. We don't really give elaborate gifts – but I do have a tiny present for you.'

'Really? What is it?'

'You'll have to wait until Christmas Day! And listen – perhaps one of the girls will invite us to her house. Both Bess and Eliza have big ovens, so we could share their roast. We could bundle Mother up and drive her over in Molly's donkey cart,' said Jem, a little doubtfully, because both sisters lived miles away.

There were certainly a flurry of letters inviting us over for Christmas, and Mother seemed excited by the idea. But when Jem and I talked it over together, it didn't seem at all practical. It was getting so cold. Mother would freeze to death on the journey, even if we wrapped her up in twenty blankets. We couldn't take her special wheeled chair too, so she would be trapped in a corner – and would there be room enough for her in any spare bed?

It was dear Janet who solved our problem. 'You must come to our house for Christmas Day,' she said. 'I'm sure Jem and Father could give Peg a chairlift to our house. We have a big oven, and you know how much my mother loves cooking. Please say you'll come, Jem and Hetty.'

I think we were both torn. I wanted to have a wonderful Christmas in our house, and that was what Jem seemed to want too. If only our walls could expand so I could invite the Maples and many other guests besides. Perhaps not my foster sisters. I'd seen a little too much of them at the funeral.

I'd have liked to invite my father for Christmas. Katherine and Mina and Ezra could have smokies and baked cod and fishy pudding back where they belonged. I'd have liked my dear friend Freda the

Female Giant to come too, though we might have to raise the ceiling specially. I'd have liked to see my pal Bertie the butcher's boy too, and he would surely bring us a fine turkey or a side of beef, but I wasn't so sure Jem would enjoy his company. And oh, most of all I'd have liked to send an invitation up to Heaven and have Mama pop down for the day. I'd make her a feast even better than manna, whatever that was. I just knew it was the only food they seemed to eat in Heaven. I paused, trying to decide what Mama would most like to eat during her visit.

'Hetty?' said Jem. He gave me a little nudge.

'I'm sorry,' he said to Janet. 'She's got that look in her eye. I think she's picturing again.'

'Don't tease me, you two,' I said, coming back to my senses. 'It's so kind of you and your family to invite us for Christmas, Janet. We'd love to come, wouldn't we, Jem?'

So that's what we did. It was all very jolly and we ate like kings. Mother particularly enjoyed herself. Mrs Maple was so kind to her. She'd made up a special chair like a throne, with extra cushions and blankets and shawls, and gave her a special Christmas meal tactfully cut into tiny pieces.

Mother was learning how to feed herself again now, though her hands were very shaky and she sometimes lost concentration halfway to her mouth. She couldn't help making a mess on the tablecloth and looked upset, but Mrs Maple patted her shoulder and said calmly, 'Don't fret, Peg dear, you're doing splendidly.'

We ate turkey, the very first time I'd tasted it. I didn't care for the live birds at all, with their weird worm-pink heads and fat feathery bodies and yellow claws. I always skirted round the turkey shed, keeping my distance. I'd had no idea that such a grotesque creature could taste so sweet and succulent. We had roast potatoes too, crisp and golden, and parsnips and carrots and small green sprouts like baby cabbages.

We ate until we were nearly bursting, but when we were offered a second serving we said yes please and Mother nodded enthusiastically. There were puddings too – a rich figgy pudding with a custard, a pink blancmange like a fairy castle, and a treacle tart with whipped cream. I could not choose which pudding I wanted because they all looked so wonderful, so I had a portion of each. This was a serious mistake, as I was wearing my first proper grown-up corset for the occasion.

I'd bought it in the hope that squeezing my stomach in with its strong whalebone might help a little bust to pop out at the top, but I remained disappointingly flat-chested – and unable to breathe properly into the bargain.

I was glad I hadn't tried to encase Mother in her own corsets. She spread comfortably underneath her loose gown. She usually fell fast asleep after a big meal, but she stayed wide awake for the present giving. The Maples gave her a specially wrapped little package. I helped her unwrap it. Mr Maple had carved her special cutlery, cleverly designed to help her manage more efficiently. The spoon had a deep bowl to prevent spillage, the fork had clever prongs for easy spearing, and the knife had a curved handle so that Mother could grip it.

She seized hold of her spoon and fork, wanting to try them out immediately, so Mrs Maple gave her another bowl of figgy pudding, even though she was already full to the brim.

Of course, Mother had no presents to give the Maples in return, but Jem and I had done our best.

Jem gave me several shillings from his farm wages and I bought them an ornament at the market – a little china model of a house, not unlike their own, with a little lumpy extra bacon room beside the chimney. There was a message written carefully across the plinth: Bless This House.

I'd wanted to find something special for Janet too, because she had been such a dear friend, so I bought her a special pen. It was a fine one, with a green mottled casing, and I rather wanted it for myself, but I decided to be generous.

The Maples were very satisfyingly pleased with their presents. Janet hugged me hard and said she would use her beautiful pen every day and think of me.

'Then at least your journal will have variety,' I said. 'You can write *Today I got up – and I love my friend Hetty!*'

Jem and Mother and I had kept our presents to give to each other at the Maples'. I didn't want to fob Mother off with yet another nightgown. I bought her a new china washing jug and bowl, white with pink babies playing all around the inside. There was also a matching chamber pot, though it seemed a shame to piddle on the little children. I kept the pot at home because it might have been embarrassing unwrapping it in company.

I couldn't wait for Jem to open his present from me. Market Jim had let me have an end roll of scarlet worsted because it had a flaw running through the weave. I cut it out carefully on the slant and avoided the flaw altogether. I'd made it into a waistcoat with pockets and brass buttons.

'Oh, I say!' said Jem, going as red as the cloth when he unwrapped the waistcoat. 'I shall look a right robin redbreast! Oh, Hetty, it's the finest waistcoat I've ever seen. I shall wear it every Sunday.'

'You don't think it's too bright?' I asked anxiously.

'Not at all – the brighter the better,' said Jem, though I'm not entirely sure he was being truthful.

'Try your waistcoat on, Jem!' said Janet.

'Yes, do – I need to see if it fits properly,' I said.

'I probably won't be able to get the buttons done up because I've had so much Christmas dinner,' said Jem – but they slid easily into place. Although it sounds dreadfully like boasting, his waistcoat looked magnificent. Even taciturn Mr Maple murmured that it was a tremendous fit.

'But I wish I knew what the time was,' I said excitedly.

They all stared at me. The Maples' brass clock was ticking steadily on the mantelpiece.

'I'd like to check the time,' I said. 'Doesn't anyone else have a timepiece, Jem? Don't gentlemen keep a pocket watch about their person?'

'You know very well I don't have a pocket watch, Hetty,' said Jem.

'Not even in your fine new waistcoat?' I said. 'Why don't you check the pockets?'

Jem stared at me, and then slid his fingers into the slim pocket at the front. His hand felt something. His mouth fell open as he drew out a gold fob watch. It wasn't real gold, it was pinchbeck, and it wasn't brand new. I'd seen it on a curiosity stall in the market and I'd bargained hard for it. It was truly a pretty ordinary watch and it didn't even have a chain, but Jem cradled it in his hand as if it were part of the crown jewels.

'Oh, Hetty,' he whispered. 'Oh, Hetty!'

'Do you like it? I thought it was time you had a watch. Now you haven't any excuse to be late home and keep supper waiting,' I joked.

'I've never had such a splendid present,' said Jem. 'Thank you so much. Thank you so very, very much. Oh dear, I wish I'd got you something as special.' He handed me a tiny parcel apologetically.

I felt it carefully. 'Is it . . . jewellery?' I asked, my heart beating fast.

Janet gave a little gasp. 'Oh, Hetty, open it!'

I picked the paper open and saw a little necklace. It was a silver sixpence with a hole bored into it so that it could hang on a dainty silver chain. 'Oh, Jem, it's lovely!' I whispered, putting it round my neck and fumbling with the clasp.

'Here, let me,' he said. 'It's an odd plain thing, I know – but you lost your last sixpence, the one I gave you as a token when you had to go off to the hospital. I thought you could keep this one hanging safe around your neck.' He fastened it in place for me. 'Perhaps it's just a silly whim. It's not very fancy like a real necklace,' he said uncertainly.

'It's perfectly lovely, Jem. I shall treasure it for ever,' I said.

Christmas With Auntie May

TRISH COOKE

IT WAS Christmas Day when Elizabeth found out about mistletoe. She had seen Ian Fuller's father kissing her mother on their doorstep. Elizabeth had remembered the time, precisely 2.15 p.m., because her mother had just, at that moment, set the correct time on Elizabeth's new watch. At 2.20 p.m. Mr Fuller had left with his twig of mistletoe and was never mentioned again. When Auntie May arrived for Christmas dinner Elizabeth would normally have jumped on her favourite aunt with Reuben but instead she stayed at the top of the stairs and looked out of the window.

'Come on,' said Nicko, holding on to Elizabeth's sleeve. 'Let's go see what Auntie May bring.'

'I already got my present,' Elizabeth said, uninterested. 'I got a make-up set,' she said, using her finger as lipstick and the window for a mirror.

'I got mine too,' said Nicko. 'But Auntie May always brings something extra . . .'

'I suppose you too big these days to give your Auntie May a kiss,' Auntie May interrupted, flipping Elizabeth over her shoulder. Auntie may liked to play and on any other day Elizabeth would have enjoyed the fun, but today her mind was on other things and *she* didn't want to kiss anyone.

Auntie May sensed there was a problem. Auntie May knew these things, and later, when everyone was playing dominoes with Uncle Isaac, she sat on the stairs with Elizabeth.

'So . . .' said Auntie May, 'what's the bottom lip for?'

Elizabeth fixed her mouth.

'What's wrong, Tizzy? Children shouldn't look so sad on Christmas day. What's wrong, you don't like the present I give you?'

'Love it,' Elizabeth smiled, remembering the make-up set.

'Den why you don't put some on, eh? Put on a happy face for your Auntie May.'

'No point,' said Elizabeth sadly.

'How you mean "No point"?'

'No point putting on a happy face if I'm not feeling happy inside,' Elizabeth said, trying not to cry.

'Sometimes,' said Auntie May, 'people have to make joke and laugh even when they not feeling happy inside. Sometimes you want to make a face that will make other people happy because if they see you sad you might make them sad too. You want to tell your Auntie May your p'oblem?'

'My problem?' Elizabeth corrected.

'What's on your mind, likkle one?'

Elizabeth thought hard. 'You know what I see today, Auntie May?'

Auntie May waited to hear what Elizabeth had seen.

'I see my mammy and Ian Fuller's daddy *kissing*.'

Auntie May did not laugh. She just cocked her head to one side and thought hard.

'And dat make you sad?' she asked eventually. Elizabeth turned away.

Auntie May kissed Elizabeth's cheek. 'Is bad to kiss?' she asked, then she kissed Elizabeth under the chin.

Elizabeth smiled because it tickled.

'Is bad to kiss?' Auntie May asked again. And then she kissed Elizabeth on her arm and on her belly and on her leg until Elizabeth began to giggle. But Auntie May did not stop there. She kissed Elizabeth again and again and again until Elizabeth could not stop laughing.

'So wha' you think is wrong wid kissin'?' Auntie May asked. Elizabeth became serious again.

'He hol' up a piece of twig like so,' Elizabeth said, holding her hand above her head. 'And he make Mammy kiss him under it. Is married they married now?'

Then Auntie May *did* laugh. 'Married?' Auntie May asked. 'You think your mammy married wid Mr Fuller?'

'Is not so?' Elizabeth asked. 'Den is why he hol' de something over dem head?'

'Because is Christmas, darling? At Christmas people does kiss under mistletoe. Is a custom.' Auntie May explained.

'A custom?' Elizabeth asked.

'A custom is a thing that people accustom' to doing. You know what I mean?'

'No,' Elizabeth said, looking puzzled.

'Is jus' something people does do at Christmas . . . not for a reason or because somebody say they mus' do it. Is something people jus' do because they want to.'

'Like giving presents?' Elizabeth asked.

'Like giving presents,' Auntie May agreed.

'Is wha' you have in your bag for us, Auntie May?' asked Nicko cheekily, peeping out of the sitting room.

'Eh eh,' said Auntie May, 'I nearly forget. Is Christmas . . .' She pursed her lips together. 'Whoever guess,' she said, 'gets a kiss.' Then she started to do silly things. First she ruffled Nicko's hair, then hopped down the stairs. The children copied. Then she kissed Auntie Lilian and ruffled her hair. The children were about to do the same but Auntie Lilian did not look amused so they did not go any closer to her.

'And that,' said Auntie May, 'is a clue to what is in my bag. Christmas . . .' and she began to make a funny face, which the children mimicked through their giggles.

'I don't know,' laughed Elizabeth.

'I can't guess,' Reuben said.

'Give us another clue,' Nicko begged.

'You have ten seconds to guess what is in my bag.' Elizabeth checked her watch and the others began to count. Everybody, even Elizabeth's mother and Auntie Lilian.

'One,' said Reuben.

'Two,' Uncle Isaac continued, making a crazy face at Auntie May.

'Three four five,' rushed Nicko.

'You're going too fast,' Elizabeth shouted. 'You have to keep in time with my watch.'

'Eight nine ten,' concluded Nicko, ignoring his bossy cousin.

'Right,' said Auntie May, reaching under the tree for her bag, 'would anyone like to have one last guess?'

Elizabeth's mother screwed up her face, which meant that she was thinking hard. 'Christmas *stupidness* . . .' she said, wiping her hands on her apron and going to the cooker.

Auntie May grinned.

'Sorry, Rosie, you wrong,' she said, pulling out an oblong-shaped box from her bag. On the back of the box was plain white, but on the other side you could see what was inside. She turned the box to the wide curious eyes.

Across the front in red lettering it said CHRISTMAS and the next word was in gold.

'CRACKERS!' the children chorused.

'Crackers, yes,' Elizabeth's mother said, shaking her head and taking out of the oven a king-sized turkey.

Auntie May opened the box of Christmas crackers and put four on the table. The children went to grab them.

'Wait, wait, wait,' Auntie May ordered, 'now let's do this thing properly.'

When Elizabeth's mother finally sat down after making sure that all the food was on the table and everybody had their serviettes, Auntie May clasped her hands together and closed her eyes. Everybody closed their eyes.

'Christmas,' Auntie May said, 'is a time for sharing, and for giving.' She opened one eye and looked at Elizabeth who was peeping too, 'and for kissing,' she smiled. The boys giggled. 'May the Lord bless this Christmas meal and we would all like to say thank you for being here today. Yes?'

'Hear hear,' agreed Uncle Isaac.

'Hear hear,' everybody agreed.

'Now the crackers, people can pull their crackers,' sang Auntie May.

'And what about me?' asked Nicko, watching Reuben pick up the cracker next to his plate. 'I want one too.'

'Pull dat one wid Reuben,' Auntie May said. Auntie Lilian shared her cracker with Uncle Isaac and Elizabeth and her mother shared theirs.

'Look' like is me alone have to pull this one,' grinned Auntie May. 'All you ready?' she asked. 'Right, PULL,' and everybody pulled their crackers together.

Reuben got a squeaky whistle. Auntie Lilian passed over their cracker because Nicko wanted a whistle too. He did not get one though. He got a key ring which he gave back to his father for his car keys. Auntie May got a pair of red lips, which she said she would wear later since she would not be able to eat if she wore them now. And Elizabeth and her mother got a green ring which Elizabeth put on.

'Now who getting married?' Auntie May teased, standing behind Elizabeth, holding a piece of mistletoe above her head. Elizabeth hid her face in her hands while Reuben and Nicko laughed into the tablecloth.

'I mus be de only one who like kissing so,' Auntie May said, putting the mistletoe above her own head.

Elizabeth got up on her chair and kissed Auntie May on the cheek.

'Whoi, whoi,' screamed Auntie May. 'Don't give me too much, people can get drunk on kiss you know,' and then she began to sing and dance around the table.

'Christmas coming once a year . . .' she sang.

'OK, OK,' said Elizabeth's mother. 'Enough, enough,' she said, covering her ears. 'Sit down, May May. Let's eat.' And Auntie May gave the children a sly look, then leaned over and kissed her sister on the cheek.

'Happy Christmas, Rosie,' she said, and Elizabeth's mother grinned.

'Happy Christmas, May May. Happy Christmas all. Now eat.'

And the Christmas table was surrounded by happy faces all enjoying their Christmas meal.

A Victorian Christmas

Many of our best-loved Christmas traditions began during the nineteenth century when Queen Victoria was on the throne.

Boxing Day

A Christmas Carol by Charles Dickens, first published in 1843, had a huge impact on its readers. The story emphasized the importance of charity at Christmastime and it became a firm tradition for wealthy Victorians to give a share of their riches to the poor. Boxing Day (26 December) got its name from the church's tradition of opening its collection boxes and giving money to the poor.

Turkey

Beef or goose was usually served for Christmas dinner as they were cheaper and more widely available than turkey. The poorer families did not own an oven and so would have their Christmas meat cooked at the local bakery. If they could not afford beef or goose they would make do with rabbit. Turkey was a luxury and, as in *A Christmas Carol*, was thought to be the ultimate in Christmas fare. Queen Victoria would no doubt have feasted on turkey, but she was also rumoured to eat roasted royal swan on Christmas Day!

Christmas Cards

The first Christmas card appeared in 1843. It was the idea of Sir Henry Cole, one of the founders of the Victoria and Albert Museum in London, and his friend and illustrator John Callcott Horsley. The central image on the postcard showed a family merrily drinking wine and celebrating, and along each edge was a drawing of people helping the poor. The cards had 'To' and 'From' on the front, as well as the standard greeting, 'A Merry Christmas and A Happy New Year to You'. The first print run was 1,000 copies and they cost one shilling each in old money!

Christmas Trees

Christmas trees had been popular in Germany since the sixteenth century but weren't widely introduced in England until after Queen Victoria's German husband,

Prince Albert, first had a tree shipped over to England in 1841. He had it decorated with candles and presented it to his wife and children. The royal family were enchanted and the fashion for Christmas trees quickly caught on. The first decorations were mostly handmade sweets and biscuits, but more and more extravagant baubles and trinkets gradually became available.

Crackers

A London confectioner called Tom Smith invented crackers in 1847 as a way of promoting his sweets and bonbons. The first crackers were simple twists of papers, but once the sweet-maker noticed their popularity at Christmas he elaborated on the novelty factor by including short love poems. Then Tom Smith made a larger version and added the 'crackle' – two strips of paper which when pulled apart produce the 'bang'. Eventually the sweets were replaced with a small toy or gift, a riddle or joke and a paper hat to create the crackers that we know and love today.

Carol Singing

Carol singing was very popular during Queen Victoria's reign, when some of the most famous carols were introduced, such as 'O Come All Ye Faithful', 'Once in Royal David's City', 'O Little Town of Bethlehem' and 'Away in a Manger'. Christmas carols are still enjoyed as an important part of Christmas by religious and non-religious people alike.

Acknowledgements

The editor and publishers gratefully acknowledge the following, for permission to reproduce copyright material for this anthology. Every effort has been made to trace copyright holders but in a few cases this has proved impossible. The editor and publishers apologize for these cases of copyright transgression and would like to hear from any copyright holder not acknowledged.

'The Christmas Party' by George Layton from *A Northern Childhood*, published in *The Balaclava Boys and Other Stories*, published by The Longman Group UK Limited 1976, copyright © George Layton 1976, reprinted by permission of Pearson Education Limited. 'The Silver Horse' by Ursula Moray Williams from *Time for a Story*, edited by Eileen Colwell, published by Puffin Books 1967, copyright © Ursula Moray Williams 1967, reproduced by permission of Curtis Brown Limited, London, on behalf of Ursula Moray Williams. 'Just Like an Angel' by Gillian Cross from *Wondrous Christmas Stories,* edited by Anne Finnis, published by Scholastic Limited 1997, copyright © Gillian Cross 1997, reprinted by permission of Scholastic Limited. 'Why the Chimes Rang' by Raymond MacDonald Alden, reprinted with permission from *A Classic Christmas Treasury,* illustrated by Christian Birmingham, copyright © 1997 by Running Press. First published in the United States by Courage Books, an imprint of Running Press Book Publishers, Philadelphia and London. First published in Great Britain by Harper-Collins Publishers Limited, London. 'The Box of Magic' by Malorie Blackman from *Magical Christmas Stories,* edited by Anne Finnis, published by Scholastic Limited 1995, copyright © Malorie Blackman 1995, reprinted by permission of Scholastic Limited. 'Christmas Is Coming' by Alison Uttley from *The Country Child,* copyright © Alison Uttley 1931, reprinted by permission of The Alison Uttley Literary Property Trust. 'Not Just for Christmas' by Rob Childs from *Wondrous*

Acknowledgements

Christmas Stories, edited by Anne Finnis, published by Scholastic Limited, copyright © Rob Childs, reprinted by permission of Celia Catchpole. 'Simon and the Snow' by Gino Alberti from *Once Upon a Christmas Time*, published by Hutchinson, copyright © Gino Alberti. Used by permission of The Random House Group Limited. 'Baboushka' retold by Caitlin Matthews from *While the Bear Sleeps: Winter Tales and Traditions*, reprinted by permission of Barefoot Books Limited, copyright © 1999 Caitlín Matthews. 'Hetty Feather's Christmas' by Jacqueline Wilson from *Emerald Star*, first published by Doubleday 2012, text copyright © Jacqueline Wilson 2012. 'Christmas With Auntie May' by Trish Cooke from *Mammy Sugar Falling Down*, published by Century Hutchinson 1989, copyright © Trish Cooke.

A Puffin Book can take you to amazing places.

WHERE WILL YOU GO?

#PackAPuffin

stories that last a lifetime

Ever wanted a friend who could take you to magical realms,
talk to animals or help you survive a shipwreck? Well, you'll find
them all in the **A PUFFIN BOOK** collection.

A PUFFIN BOOK will stay with you **forever**.
Maybe you'll read it again and again, or perhaps years from now
you'll suddenly **remember** the moment it made you **laugh** or
cry or simply see things **differently**. Adventurers **big** and **small**,
rebels out to **change** their world, even a mouse with a **dream**
and a spider who can spell – these are the characters who
make **stories** that last a **lifetime**.

Whether you love animal tales, war stories or want to
know what it was like growing up in a different time and place,
the **A PUFFIN BOOK** collection has a story for you
– you just need to decide where you want to go next . . .